SOLOMON'S QUEST:

THE COMPLETE ADVENTURES
OF JOHN SOLOMON, VOLUME 3

H . BEDFORD-JONES

SOLOMON'S QUEST

THE ADVENTURES OF
JOHN SOLOMON, VOLUME 3

H. BEDFORD-JONES

STEEGER BOOKS • 2019

TABLE OF CONTENTS

SOLOMON'S QUEST

CHAPTER I

A STRING OF BEADS

BEING A ship's physician is no sinecure, especially on a P. & O. liner bound from Liverpool to the ends of the earth. The lascars may develop anything from cholera to mumps, the passengers usually develop mal de mer, and the stokehold is apt at developing queer things caused by fire bars which rip open a lazy stoker's scalp. So, when old England faded out behind us, I looked only for the usual routine of labour.

We had the usual passenger list of tourists, officers and their women folk, cub officials for Mombasa and Bombay, and so forth. I had no longing for their society, not having become acclimated to the breed of official Britisher who has not yet done things in the world. The cub who is "going out" for the first time is always an insufferable ass, though I will say that a few years in service make a tolerable man of him.

However, let us have the agony over and done with. My name is Walter Firth—I am an M.D. from Johns Hopkins, and obtained my berth in the P. & O. line through the influence of one of my professors there. Two years of it had thoroughly sickened me of the job, and I was already figuring on saving enough with which to get back to Buffalo and buy into a practice, when this eventful voyage completely flung me off my bases—together with some other people a good deal more important than Walter Firth, M.D.

I am not at all certain that my story will meet with any credence. It is too terrible, too melodramatic, too improbable.

My only reason for writing it is that the world may have a final record of a great man; I am not the hero of the story, for I only used the brain and thews God gave me in my own blind and blunt way. It is for and of *him* that I write—the little pudgy man with the mild sky-blue eyes. I loved him, and I would cheerfully give ten years of my life could I have brought him whole out of that hell-hole. I never even learned enough to draw tight the loosened threads of inference, so that I can but write the story as it happened from my own viewpoint.

On my second voyage I had laid off at Alexandria with a broken leg, and to while away the time I hired a Frenchman to teach me Arabic—the true name of which is Arbi. I learned it villainously; but what with French and natives and officers, my knowledge improved and I picked it up quite decently by the time this eventful cruise took place. And there is quite a distinction between the words "voyage" and "cruise," please note.

We were half a day from Gibraltar, and all was going well. The usual duties of my position were accomplished: tourists, civilians, and old ladies, had found their sea legs: an outbreak of "bubonic" among the lascars had proved to be chickenpox; the usual shaking down had formed the passengers into cliques and coteries. One man I had noticed who said nothing to anyone and took his meals in his stateroom—a well-wrapped little man, who always sat by himself in the sun.

His hair was grey almost to whiteness, his face quite expressionless despite its deep lines of suffering, his eyes very blue and round. He always smoked a cheap clay pipe and was attended by a native servant in European dress, an Afghan, I thought.

Half a day from Gib, then, I was hurriedly summoned from dinner by a white-lipped deck steward, who whispered me to fetch my instruments to a spare second-class cabin, that a man was stabbed. Obtaining my instrument case, I hastened to the cabin in question, and was admitted by the ship's second officer.

"Too late, I'm afraid," he remarked. "The beggar's kicked off by now."

"What's up?" I asked quickly, leaning over the injured man. "Who did it?"

He told me, while I examined the man. The latter was dark-skinned, not a lascar, but a member of the coal gang, and had been stabbed under the sixth rib—a terrible stab. He was done for, and lay in a coma.

There had been a fight, it seemed. This man and the Afghan servant of my clay-pipe smoker had mixed it up near the rail; the Afghan had gone overboard with his throat cut, but had killed his enemy in turn. The case was kept quiet, of course, but it was very curious how the servant of a first-cabin passenger should get mixed up with a coal heaver.

"Has the passenger been informed?" I asked, staring down at the scarcely breathing native.

"Yes—the dirty little Cockney!" and the second officer uttered a smothered oath. "Never turned a hair— Hello! Is the beggar coming to?"

I leaned over the dying man again, for he had opened his eyes and was staring up at me, gasping terribly for breath, one hand clutching at his waist cloth. As I tried to quiet him, he twisted up, and his fingers pressed something into my hand. A horrible broken whisper in Arabic bubbled from his lips:

"The blue bead—the—the blue-bead of—"

He died upon the word.

Looking down at the object he had forced upon me with his death struggle, I saw that it was a bead of blue lacquer or enamel, a half inch square, with a hole pierced from one side to the other. Upon one face was set into the enamel a golden thread, exactly like the short-hand symbol for "things." It was the Arabic letter "fa," corresponding to our own "f," but did not have the usual vowel dot above.

I stared at it in wonder, but as neither I nor the second officer could make anything of it, I thrust the thing into my pocket as a souvenir. Barely had I done so, when a cabin steward came running, and panted that I was wanted at once by a Mr. Solomon, outside upper-deck cabin B56.

"He's the Afghan's master," volunteered the second officer.

"Solomon, eh?" I said, gathering up my things. "A Hebrew, I suppose?"

"Not a bally bit of it. Pure Cockney. Tip me off if there's anything to this affair more than a lascar row."

I nodded and hurried away after the cabin steward, and so gained my introduction to John Solomon, the queerest man I ever met—and I was going to say the most terrible, but that would be untrue. The most terrible was Colonel Parrish.

Seen without his enveloping steamer rug, Solomon was a podgy little man, though his clothes hung loosely upon him. I found him smoking his eternal clay pipe, carpet slippers on his feet, and a tarboosh cocked jauntily over one ear. Naturally, at first I thought him a bit daft. He waved me to the other chair and took out a little red notebook, his wide blue eyes surveying me rather keenly.

"Doctor Firth?" and his accent was, indeed, Cockney. "You're an American, sir?"

"I am," and I fear that I betrayed some wonder at his odd aspect.

"Dang it, sir," and he sighed as if in weariness, "so they've been an' murdered that 'ere Afghan o' mine! The second officer said as 'ow another man was 'urt, so I says, 'John, let's talk wi' the doctor,' just like that. There ain't no 'arm in 'avin' a bit o' talk, as the old gentleman said when 'e met the 'ousemaid in the entryway."

"You seem to take your servant's death pretty callously," I said, nettled. "What do you want of me?"

"Callously, is it?" He removed his pipe, staring hard at me for a moment. "Doctor Firth, that 'ere Afghan was as near a brother to me as any brown man could be to a white. But I 'as me own way o' showin' me grief, sir. Mournin' ain't intended for the outside, but for the inside, I says. Now, Doctor Firth, if you'll be so good as to tell me about that 'ere murderer—"

"He's dead," I returned, and told how the man had died, without mention of the blue bead. Solomon cocked his head on one side, watching me as he listened.

"An' didn't 'e say nothin' before 'e died, sir?"

"A mutter of Arabic—nothing to do with the case," I rejoined curtly, and repeated the man's words, in Arabic.

The effect was astonishing. Solomon's eyes widened and he stiffened in his chair, staring at me. Then he repeated the words in English—"The blue bead!"

It was my turn to be surprised, for I had not translated. This absurd little Cockney who travelled first cabin with an Afghan servant actually knew Arabic! What was more, upon recovering from his first amazement, he leaned forward and opened the red notebook, writing rapidly with a pencil. And the writing was in Arabic!

"It's 'im! I knowed it!" Solomon snapped the notebook shut and leaned back, resuming his stare and his pipe together. He seemed almost dazed. "It's 'im, as I thought was dead an' buried a good year ago! Dang it, now I am in for it an' no mistake, as the old gentleman said when the 'ousemaid begun a-cryin'."

I gazed at him in some perplexity, wondering if the man was crazed.

"What are you talking about, Solomon?" I demanded sharply. "Who's your 'him'?"

He stared slightly, then drew another deep sigh. There was a weariness in his wide blue eyes, as of a man who sees his labour failed and himself doomed to begin it anew. Quietly, he slipped the little red notebook into his pocket, still looking at me.

"Now, Doctor Firth," he said slowly, "I suppose as 'ow you didn't see nothin' o' that there blue bead?"

He was evidently in deep earnest, and he was certainly not crazy. I began to imagine that there was some mystery about that peculiar bead, after all; without replying, I took it from my pocket, eyeing him narrowly. I saw his eyes widen a trifle, but at sight of it he merely nodded slightly and shifted his gaze to my face.

"Now, Doctor Firth," said he, "you're a young man, so to speak, and you know Arbi, but I'll wager me 'at you can't be a-tellin' me what that 'ere bead's made of!"

No more could I. The thing was heavy; from the thread of golden wire spelling the Arabic symbol it might have been a sort of cloisonne, yet it was not. I shook my head in puzzled negation.

"Well, sir, that 'ere bead was made a mortal long time ago, Doctor Firth; it was that! You've heard o' them there tiles the Arabs used to make, about the twelfth century? It's a lost art, as the 'ousemaid said when the butler asked 'er for a kiss. But that 'ere bead was made at that werry time, sir. I'll give you a hundred quid for that bead, sir."

Again Solomon had me all at sea. A hundred pounds—five hundred dollars—for this little atom of blue lacquer! As he spoke, he drew out a wallet bulging with real United States money, and it almost made me homesick to look at it.

"Take it," I said abruptly, handing him the bead. "I don't want your money. If it's any good to you, you're welcome."

He promptly shoved away the pocket-book, thanked me politely, then put a hand to his coat pocket. From it he drew a string of beads—exactly like this blue one, except that they were of all colours, strung on a bit of common red twine. Carefully untying the string ends, he threaded the blue bead, drew a deep sigh, and shoved them into his pocket.

Quite naturally, I was amazed. If he had paid five hundred dollars for each of them, they represented a tidy fortune. But— what about the double murder?

"Look here, Solomon," I exclaimed, "where did that blue bead come from? Did it start the row between your Afghan and that lascar?"

He nodded calmly: "Yes, sir, it did that. Only, 'e wasn't no lascar, so to speak. That 'ere beggar, Doctor Firth, was a genuine

Arab. If I may make so bold as to ask, sir, did 'e 'ave a red scar over 'is 'eart?"

"Yes," I nodded. "A cicatrice resembling a vaccination mark. What was it?"

"Ah, I wonder now!" The mild blue eyes held all the wondering innocence of a baby's. "But Doctor Firth, you're by way o' bein' a fine upstandin' man; you are that. I'm mortal afraid, sir, you'd better watch out werry 'ard wi' both eyes, just like that. There's them a-comin' aboard at Gibraltar who'll be mortal 'ard 'it by the death o' that there Arab, Doctor Firth."

He was warning me, that much was plain, yet I felt unreasonably angered with him. So vacuous were those blue eyes, so devoid of expression, that they irritated me.

"You're a queer man, Solomon," I said, a trifle contemptuously. "And I'm afraid your brains are a bit addled. I've nothing to fear from the death of that Arab and since you seem so anxious to get that blue bead, it's a whole lot more likely that you set your Afghan on the man. In fact, I intend reporting as much to the captain."

I watched him narrowly, but the shot made no hit. He only chuckled and held a vesta to his bubbling pipe.

"Try it," he returned calmly. "But I like you, Doctor Firth, I do that; 'cause why, you're a man as don't ask questions, an' grey-eyed men as don't ask questions are mortal good men to tie up to. Now sir, you watch out. I knows nothing and I says nothing except just that—you watch out."

"But what for, you idiot?" I broke forth angrily. "I've done nothing!"

He wagged his head solemnly.

"I knows nothing and I says nothing whatsoever, which is the secret o' success, Doctor Firth, sir. Only, you and the second officer took care of that 'ere Arab, an' if that blue bead ain't found on 'im, why, one of you 'as it. That's all, sir. Don't you go a-tellin' as you give it to John Solomon, mind that."

"I certainly shall," I retorted, rising in helpless despair of the man. "I'll make my report to the captain, most certainly; otherwise, of course, my lips are sealed. And I'm much mistaken if you don't hear more of it, my man."

"Try it, sir," he chuckled, blowing out a cloud of smoke. "But mind me words—you watch out. Just like that. You watch out, Doctor Firth—but if so be as you need 'elp, why you just come to John Solomon. Thankee kindly, sir."

In mingled wrath and bewilderment, I left him and sought out the captain, to whom I made a report of the whole business, with all Solomon had said. To my intense surprise, the captain, who was an R.N., and old in the service, forbade my making any written report of the case, nor would he assign any reasons.

"If Solomon told you to watch out, doctor," he said dryly, "you do it, and do it mighty sharp. That's all I can say—"

"But confound it, captain—I'm no child! Who is this man, Solomon? A stockholder, a lunatic, or a king in disguise?"

The captain looked at me, and his eyes wrinkled up about the comers.

"He is a Cockney, Firth—a fat little Cockney, born and bred in Wapping, and for thirty years, until a year or so ago, he has conducted a shipchandler's store in Port Said. If you want to know more, ask him."

I knew the captain pretty well, and shut up. There was something behind his words which mystified me; he knew a lot more about Solomon than he cared to say. I concluded that the Cockney was favoured by the company, perhaps having worked for them, and so let the whole affair drop *pro tem.*

We made Gib that night, and, having the mails aboard, left the Rock the next morning. Mindful of Solomon's words, I scanned the half-dozen passengers who came aboard, but none of them looked in the least suspicious. Only one of them was remarkable; he was a man named Lionel Parrish, and attracted me because of his tremendous power of face and physique. Being a strong man myself, I like men who are my equals in body.

This man Parrish was something better than my equal, I

conjectured. He was an inch taller than I, which would make him six feet two, and carried himself like a soldier. Above his magnificent chest and shoulders was set a head such as I have never seen on a man since. He was deeply bronzed, and his eyes were a vivid brown, deep-set and piercing—eyes of mastery, and very cruel. His features were aquiline, proud even to haughtiness, while from his lean jaw a brown beard stuck out forkwise, so that I thought of King Svein Forkbeard when I looked at him. And he looked a king, every inch of him.

It was with something of a shock that I found he travelled second cabin.

However, to get along with my story. We were three hours out of Gibraltar when I was called below in a hurry. I found the second officer dead—struck by a falling trunk as he was getting some luggage stowed away properly. His neck had been broken instantly. That was at six bells in the afternoon—three o'clock.

My report was written out. I was dressing for dinner, and had just picked up my razor when I noticed a slight discolouration along the edge of the blade. I looked at it more closely, then took it to a microscope. After that, I made two simple tests, and sat down suddenly with a cold hand gripping at my heart.

As any physician knows, there are three—and possibly more—poisons which will kill a human being instantly, and leave absolutely no trace. For obvious reasons the names of these are never made public; I can only say that my razor had been carefully edged with one of them, and at the slightest scratch, perhaps without a scratch even, I was a dead man. No wonder I felt sick.

It came over me in a flash what Solomon had said. The second officer had taken care of the dead Arab; he was now dead himself. I had assisted, and I had come too close to death for my own comfort. There was no use in questioning the stewards, as I knew well; only one man on board could give me any satisfaction, and I was savagely determined to get it. So I rang for the cabin steward.

"Go to Mr. Solomon's stateroom—outside upper deck, B56—and inform him that I am dining with him. Then have dinner served in his cabin for two."

"Yes, sir."

I closed the razor, horribly nervous, and wrapped it in a towel. Without dressing, I put my revolver in my coat pocket, left my cabin, and set forth to find Solomon.

"And, my man, you're going to talk, or I'll show you something!" I said inwardly, as I came to B56. I was angered clear through, and more frightened than I cared to admit.

CHAPTER II

I LEARN SOMETHING

"**C**OME IN, sir, and werry glad I am to see you."

I slammed the door behind me, and shoved the towel at Solomon.

"Open that—and be mighty careful."

He obeyed me, then stared at the razor in wonder, as I explained the manner of its poisoning. He seemed very much perturbed; when I had finished, he took up the razor, went to the port, and heaved it out. Then he returned to his chair, white-faced.

"Ugh! It fair gives me the 'orrors, it does that!"

"I'll give you more than that," I said, eyeing him. "I came here to dine with you, Solomon, and you're going to talk. Understand? There's something behind all this, something perfectly damnable, and I'm going to get at it. You know. Don't lie to me! You know, and it's connected with that cursed blue bead. Now come across with it."

He reached into his pocket and pulled out a plug of tobacco, which he carefully began to whittle into his clay pipe. I had barely finished, however, when the stewards appeared with their folding table and dinner, and our conversation was cut short for the present. Later, I was glad of it; that terrible razor had unnerved me, and I might have undertaken to force the information from Solomon—something which no man alive could do. He seemed not to resent my taking charge of things.

"Now, sir," he said genially, when I had dismissed the stewards, "let's 'ave a quiet bit o' food, then we'll 'ave our talk. Werry glad I am as things 'as come about as they 'as, Doctor Firth. I've 'ad me eye on you since we left Liverpool."

With which astonishing bit of information he settled down at the table, and we discussed everything but the subject in hand. I calmed down gradually. The more I saw of this amazing little man, the deeper I found him. Before dinner was over I was heartily ashamed of the way in which I had gone at him.

"Now, sir," and he waved aside my proffered cigar in favour of his pipe, "I know your 'ole 'istory, Doctor Firth. When I come aboard at Liverpool, I says, 'John, there's the werry man as you need,' just like that. Before we'd left the Thames I'd 'ad your 'istory—beggin' your pardon for the liberty, sir. There's one thing, howsoever, as only you can tell me, sir. Are you a Christian man, Doctor Firth?"

Fortunately for myself, as it proved, I resisted the irritation welling up within me. The man was in deadly earnest, no question about that. I had a vague suspicion that behind the absurdity of his words and manner there lay something definite. It was only a suspicion, but it showed a glimmering of sense in my head.

"Depends on what you mean," I growled, puzzled. "I'm not what you might call a religious man, but I'm not like some doctors I know. If it came to a distinction between being a Christian and being a Buddhist, I'm a Christian. What is it to you? What are you driving at?"

"Them as asks questions gets less'n they asks, I says," returned Solomon, and heaved a sigh again. He seemed to have an inexhaustible store of them. "Doctor Firth, I'll 'ave to go about this in me own way, bein' as it's a long story. I like you fine, sir, I do that; an' if you're the man I think you are, why, I 'opes we'll 'ave times ahead."

Not being able to make him out in the least, I relapsed into silence and gave him his head. He drummed on the table with his fingers for a moment, watching me, then drew from his pocket the red notebook I had previously seen. Pawing it over, he finally found his place and handed the book to me.

"Read that, Doctor Firth. It'll save a mortal sight o' talk. Talk is a werry fine thing, I says, in its place; but its place ain't alongside the printed word, says I."

Then it was that I learned a most astounding thing. Here is the entry from the notebook, as I copied it later, verbatim:

> *Parrish, Lionel.* Lieut. U.S.A. Dismissed service '04, conduct unbecoming gent. Morocco, leading Riffians; Arabia, colonel in Turkish army; prefect of Senussiyeh; beat Bulgars Adrianople; built El Woda'a, captured by J.S. Suicide; poison.
>
> Age at death, 35. Moslem name, Abu Talib, the Kadiri. Unmarried. Rumour suicide was fraud. Investigate at once. *Memo.*—May be concerned in affair of beads.

The words ran into a blur before my eyes. I remembered the lion-like man who had come aboard at Gibraltar that morning—Lionel Parrish! Into what web of intrigue and mystery was I being drawn? Bewildered, I looked at Solomon in a mute question.

"The werry same, sir," he said slowly, answering my thought. "That's 'im as come aboard us. A renegade 'e is, a dirty renegade, Doctor Firth!"

There was absolute fear in the man's voice, a fact which did not appreciate until I later discovered his iron fortitude. Yet I could not believe him.

"That man a renegade?" I asked slowly. "Solomon, he looks more like a king among men! You must be barking up he wrong tree—"

"You listen 'ere, sir." He leaned forward, his wide blue eyes staring into mine. "I'm a-goin' to trust you, 'cause dry, I ain't got no one else an' I like you fine, sir. You listen 'ere."

And with that Solomon spoke steadily and solemnly of things incredible. I knew already that there was a secret order of fighting Moslem monks called the Senussiyeh with half northern Africa in its grip, holding the British, Italians, and French in

positive fear. That is no secret, even among travellers. The Senussiyeh, with its ten million members, its untold wealth, its secret
fortified cities in the desert—this monastic order is the back-
bone of Islam to-day, and will make history to-morrow.

Here is Solomon's tale, in brief. Parrish was a *mokkhadem,* or
prefect, in that secret order, and had become a Moslem years ago.
With all the power of the Senussiyeh at his back, he had built a
stronghold called El Woda'a. The Gate of Farewell, not far from
Medina on the Red Sea. His intention was to seize Mecca and
Medina, the holy cities of the Moslem world, grasp all Arabia,
and restore Islam as a world power.

He had all but succeeded, when Solomon stepped in, backed
by the alarmed sultan at Constantinople, and smashed the
Senussiyeh in Arabia. Parrish, being captured, took a seeming poison, and was left for dead. Evidently, he had used some
cunning drug which left the life in him.

Now, all this was like a rigmarole from a nightmare at first.
But after half an hour I believed John Solomon implicitly. For
all its incredible absurdity, the man's tale was backed up by
proofs indisputable; he showed me jewelled orders from half
the knighthoods in Europe, for example. It was staggering, but
it was true. This Cockney was better than a king.

In order that I myself may find credence. I will here set down
what I learned then and later about John Solomon, though
I never learned much in detail. As the captain had said, he
was ostensibly a ship-chandler in Port Said. In reality, he had
conducted an organization reaching through Moslem lands—a
secret organization of which he alone was the head and genius. It
managed everything from gun-running to private wars; within
the last year, John had voluntarily disbanded it and taken refuge
in the United States.

He had come to grips with the Porte itself, had won his
game, and had wisely gone away to let the storm settle. Also, it
appeared, to recover his shattered health. The fine threads of his
private organization had reached out through half the East; he

had aided kings and causes, had fought princes and principles, and he took a keen delight in the sheer playing of the game itself.

As may be gathered, John Solomon was more than a personality—he was a genius, a Talleyrand of the back stairs, a Napoleon of the Eastern underworld. He had millions in the Crédit Lyonnais, and adherents by the hundred. But the East is a mass of intrigue. At different times he had outpointed both the Senussiyeh and the Porte, and in venturing back to the lands of Islam he was playing with death—and knew it.

So much for John Solomon, the deadly enemy of Lionel Parrish. Contrasting the pudgy little ship-chandler with the regal, proud, virile adventurer, I could not but wonder at it all. Yet Solomon's hatred of Parrish lay in the fact that the American had gone over to the faith of Islam, was a renegade.

After his great failure and seeming suicide, Parrish had been in sore straits. The Senussiyeh does not countenance failure. Yet, because Parrish was a prefect and one of its strongest men, the order had retained him at one of its secret north African cities, and now was giving him a chance to win back his lost reputation.

Just how, John would not say. It concerned that string of beads, but he refused to explain at the time, because it was hard on midnight before he had me finally convinced that his story was true, and that he was the thing he said. If I had needed any further conviction, it lay in the poisoned razor.

"I'll 'ave to get that 'ere Parrish off your trail, sir," said John finally. To this end he wrote a brief note, stating that he had the blue bead, signed his name, and laid it by. Parrish knew he was aboard, and John intended to slip the ship at Malta.

It was a vast relief to know that I need fear no more poisoned razors, and on finding that it was midnight, we parted. Then, and not until then, Solomon sprang his big surprise.

"Doctor Firth," he said solemnly, "if so be as you knew as 'ow you was a-goin' to do your duty as a Christian gentleman, sir, would you throw up this 'ere job?"

I looked hard at him.

"What do you mean?"

"Well, let me be puttin' of it in another way, as the old gentleman said when 'e discharged 'is butler by a-kickin' of 'im out. If so be as you stood a mortal good chance of gettin' killed, sir, an' a mortal poor chance o' makin' your fortune, all along o' doing your honest Christian duty—would you throw up this 'ere job to do it, Doctor Firth?"

He meant it, and meant a lot more than he said. After learnin' what I had learned that evening there was only one thing to say, and I said it. Then Solomon asked me to pass my word that I would resign the next morning, to take effect at Port Said. I did so. With that, he promised to communicate with me at Port Said—and we parted.

As may be imagined, I slept little that night. Reflecting upon my pending resignation, I saw clearly that Solomon had offered me a chance at one of his big underground affairs. Having heard his story, I knew there was a big risk, and a probable big reward. It must have been a tremendous affair which could draw him from his haven of safety in the United States, back to the East so pregnant with danger to him.

However, I turned in my resignation to the captain next morning, with no explanation. The captain looked at me searchingly, then nodded.

"Very good, sir. I am sorry to lose you, Doctor Firth, but—well, here's good luck to you and a straight passage with your new captain!"

From which I gathered that he understood exactly what had happened.

I had counted on learning a good deal from Solomon about those beads of mystery, but counted without the Cockney. At Malta, John Solomon vanished. I could have sworn that he did not go ashore, yet he disappeared. Parrish continued as a passenger, though seldom in sight, and I found that he was booked to Alexandria.

More than once I cursed myself for a fool. It is no easy matter

to throw up an easy berth for mighty uncertain prospects, at
the bidding of a fat Cockney. I would not have been tempted to
break my word, however, had it not been for Molly Quaintance.

How she got on the bridge was a mystery to me; she came
aboard at Malta, and I found her laughing with the captain that
evening. The old captain always had a soft place in his heart for
pretty girls, however, and Molly was more than pretty. She was
tall, slender, and dark of skin, with very black hair. Her eyes
were like the violet night-mist out of the Niagara gorge, and
her features were as straight and regular and wonderfully handsome as—as—well, as those of Lionel Parrish. I can think of no
finer thing with which to compare them, despite the man's devil
heart. Best of all, Molly had a tremendous amount of imagination grappled down by the anchor of common sense.

The captain introduced us, and, like a true Britisher, he said
I was from Buffalo, somewhere in the wild West. Then he went
away, being a sensible man. Molly and I went into the chart
house and settled down on the lockers.

"You're the only other American on board," I said, "except
those cinema people—"

"Cut it out," she broke in, laughing. "Talk United States, for
Heaven's sake! I notice you haven't adopted any accent, Doctor
Fifth, so when you mean the movies, don't say the cinema."

"You win," I laughed. "May I smoke? Thanks. You're a tour-
ist, of course?"

"You don't catch tourists on these mail packets, do you? No,
I'm a trained nurse."

"Oh!" I said and looked at my cigar carefully. "I see."

"I'll give you another guess," and her eyes seemed to flood
with laughter on a sudden, as I looked up into them.

"Well," I replied cautiously, "I suppose you're going out to do
mission work among the heathen, Miss Quaintance. I don't see
why they always send the prettiest—"

"You're wrong," she exclaimed quickly. "But I'll have mercy on
you, because you're an American. I'm going out to Aden, where

my uncle will meet me. You see, I'm alone in the world, and my uncle is doing some important archaeological work and exploring among the sand-buried cities in the interior of Arabia—"

"What's his name?" I asked quickly.

"Professor Eli Graves, University of Chicago. He's been there a year now."

I nodded, having read his books and heard a good deal about him, like everyone else.

"Maybe he knows what he's doing," I grunted, looking straight at her, "but anyone who would take an unprotected girl into the middle of Arabia ought to be shot. Especially if she's a girl like you.

"Oh, this is different!" she exclaimed eagerly. "You know, the Turks have almost no hold on Arabia beyond Medina. Uncle Eli has conducted negotiations between the British and the emirs of the interior, and is very strong with the Arabs. They allow him to go everywhere, help him in every way possible—"

"I know all that," I said impatiently. "Why does he drag you into it?"

"For several reasons." She settled back comfortably, her fingers playing with a long chain which ran from her neck to her waist. Already I felt as though I had known her for years, perhaps because we were two Americans in a dry and barren ship, where no tourists were. At any rate, she seemed to like my sudden interest in her affairs.

"For one reason, he wanted some things which no one else could be trusted to bring him," she explained gravely. "Then, my experience in charity nursing in Chicago will do a lot of good among the Arabs—"

She ceased suddenly as I leaned forward, astounded: I suppose my amazement must have shown in my face. For, set on that slender silver chain about her neck, were three or four square beads—exactly the same as those which Solomon had shown me, and of different colours! The lacquer and slender thread of gold in each was unmistakable.

"Great Scott!" I said slowly. "What are those things—where did you get them?"

She stared at me in some surprise, a little flush in her dark face.

"Those beads, you mean? Uncle Eli got them in Cairo, ten years ago. There are five—rather peculiar things, aren't they? He gave them to me when I was a little girl, and I had them set on this chain. This is one of the things he ordered me to bring to him, and keep carefully, though I can't imagine why."

Beyond a doubt she spoke truth, for here was a girl in whom there was no guile. The very openness with which she wore them showed her ignorance of what they were. I gave an inward groan of helplessness, but, like a flash, I remembered Parrish and that blue bead, for which three men had died within two days. The Arab, with the mark of the Senussiyeh on his breast; Parrish, a prefect of that devilish monastic order—"

"Look here, Miss Quaintance," I said earnestly, "get those beads out of sight and keep 'em there. No, I'm not joking. I can't tell you why, and don't quite know myself; but I do know that if you're seen wearing them, they'll never reach your uncle, and neither will you, likely enough. Put them away, please."

Her eyes widened a little, searching my face. She must have read my terrible earnestness in my voice and face, for she quietly tucked the chain inside her waist. At the same instant there was a step behind us, and I turned to see Lionel Parrish in the port doorway. He looked at me as I rose, his brown eyes as cold as ice.

"Ah—I beg your pardon, sir," he said, bowing slightly, and his eyes flitted to the girl, then back to my face. "I thought the captain had the deck—"

"You'll find him on the upper bridge," I said curtly. "How did you get here? Passengers are not allowed on the bridge deck."

The man looked at me for a long moment, and never in my life had I felt such a horrible sensation as I did beneath his cold gaze. He impressed me as a thing, not as a man; a thing, a machine of indomitable power, driven by a relentless will; an inhuman, steel-strung thing against which no mere man could stand and live to tell of it. And that impression was exactly correct, as I found later.

"Your pardon, sir," he replied evenly, his voice like a bronze bell in its clear quality. Like a bell, too, it had an after ring; a deadly note which left me chilled. "The mistake was unintentional, I assure you."

He bowed and vanished outside. I sank down on a chair, and found my brow thick with sweat. In that moment I believed every word Solomon had told me of this man.

"Who was that, Doctor Firth?" and the girl's voice seemed to waken me. "What a terribly handsome man! Do you know him?"

"No," I muttered thickly. "No, I hope to Heaven I never see him again, either! Now come with me, please. We will take that chain to the purser, and you'll get it from him at Aden, if you please."

"But—why—" She rose, looking at me with her level-eyed gaze, her face puzzled.

"Don't ask me," I broke out. "I don't know, Miss Quaintance, and that's the truth. But do as I say, please! Come!"

Well, she agreed at last. As we went below, I knew that I was going to have a stiff pull leaving the boat at Port Said, despite my pledged word. 'Cause why, as Solomon would have said, I wanted to go on as far as Aden, and wanted it very much indeed.

CHAPTER III

I MEET SOLOMON

DESPITE ITS deadly monotony to the old traveller, Port Said is a wonderful place, more French than British, and more Arab than French. As I stood out in front of the "Savoy" on the Quai François Joseph and watched the old ship pull down the Ismail Basin for Aden and the Far East, I felt tremendously lonely.

The harbour was full of ships, and the streets were full of people; British officials, sweet young things from America trailing after Cook guides, Iowa farmers and New York's gilded youth elbow to elbow, and others, not to mention Maltese and Arabs and camels and donkeys which are a lot more valuable than mere people in the East. But I looked out beyond it all to the great statue of De Lesseps, standing lone and high above the breakwater, and felt miserable. So I went back into the hotel bar and showed the French bar-keep how to mix a real horse's neck. He could not understand why it had no fire water in it.

It seemed to me that I had been a simple fool. I was out of a soft job, landed in Port Said with a hundred pounds to my credit, and utterly dependent on the vague promises of a blue-eyed pudgy Cockney. It was absurd. Molly Quaintance was still aboard the ship, and I had kept my word to Solomon after a mighty hard fight. I kicked myself mentally and cursed myself outwardly.

"Never a word from Solomon," I mused gloomily, stirring my horse's neck. "If it wasn't for the mystery of those beads, I'm hanged if I wouldn't recall my resignation and let the Cockney go fish for another sucker!"

At my right hand, leaning on the bar, stood a slender, soldierly Arab, dressed in extra-fine tailored clothes of the latest European cut. I noticed him only because his face was pockmarked rather deeply, yet handsome in spite of it. In my mood of loneliness I did not want to go to my room in the hotel, so, as it was early afternoon, I went down the quay to the P. & O. office, took a chair behind the desk, and chinned with the clerk—an old retired sea captain who had served here in Port Said for five years.

I asked him about John Solomon, but he had never heard the name before, so we talked about everything in general, and how badly the Peninsular & Oriental line was managed in particular. After half an hour a man came in and asked rates to Aden. He was the same pock-marked Arab I had noticed in the hotel bar, but I thought nothing of it. When closing time came, the agent and I split a bottle of beer, and I settled down in the hotel lobby to go over the latest Reuter's. While I was at it, along came that same Arab and settled into a chair opposite. I began to take notice of him, and, after a bit, caught him eyeing me furtively. When he saw me watching him, he moved on and disappeared.

Perhaps this started it, but for the rest of the evening I had an uneasy feeling that I was followed. Remembering that poisoned razor, I grew nervous to the extent of taking a comer chair in the lobby and smoking the hours away until bedtime. At ten o'clock I drifted back to the bar, found it empty, and got another horse's neck. I paid for it with a five-franc piece; as the French bartender handed me my change, a folded slip of paper came into my hand with the coins.

"Read in private, m'sieu, and destroy," murmured the bartender, then turned as two tourists entered.

I felt a pleasant thrill of excitement. It began to look as though I had entered into an Oriental mystery, after all! Putting change and note into my pocket, I left the bar and sought my room, where, with the blinds drawn and the door locked, I opened the note and found my keenest anticipations fulfilled. After I had read it, I remember d that three men had died in two days for a blue bead—and that thought sobered me completely. Here is the note, which was unsigned, but in Solomon's copperplate writing:

> Meet friend in front of Duane ten to-morrow. Am hurt, but recovering. You will not return to hotel. Get mail and cables for me at Crédit Lyonnais.

Thoughtfully enough, I held the note to a match and watched it crisp out to a black ash. My despondency had vanished abruptly, for in the curt message there was more than a hint of startled action, of nervous energy, and I went to bed with the thought that things were going to move fast. Had I guessed what those things were, and the manner of their moving, my slumbers would have been a good deal less sound, I verily believe.

As all my things were in a small handbag, I paid up and left the hotel by nine in the morning, took a tram ride to the Arab quarters and back, and got off again at the "Savoy." The custom-house is directly opposite, on the quay, but I walked around to the Rue du Nil to the Crédit Lyonnais and got Solomon's mail and cables—quite a bunch of them, which were given to me without any questions. It looked strongly as if my description had been widely circulated.

By that time it was nearly ten, so I came back to the Duane and stood on the comer to light a cigar. I had not a ghost of an idea whom I was to meet; the quay was crowded with people and cabs, brilliant with fezzes and burnooses and uniforms. As I flung away my match, a one-legged beggar crowded in with extended hand.

"Pity the poor, effendi!" he whined, in French, then followed it instantly with a sibilant whisper: "Are you followed? Take the cab to your right—the black horse."

Amazed though I was, I reached into my pocket for a coin, and nodded.

"A pock-marked Arab in European clothes is watching me," I returned, as I passed him a franc, "or was last night."

He fell on the coin with a howl of thanks, grovelling in a disgusting fashion. I turned and saw a cab standing a few yards away, the horse a fine black. As I approached, the driver touched his cap and flung open the door.

"Waiting, m'sieu," he said simply, and, realizing that I was being thoroughly taken care of, I threw in my bag and followed it. Barely had we begun to move, when I heard a sudden uproar, and looked out to see my pock-marked Arab engaged in angry abuse with the one-legged beggar. Even as my gaze caught them, the Arab struck the beggar angrily; there was a yell and a swirl of men, and the efficient little brown constables swarmed down as we drove away.

I have told all this in some detail merely to show the efficient and astounding methods and men of John Solomon. He had left our mail boat at Malta, yet had evidently come to Port Said ahead of me—which was some mystery in itself. However, he had done it, and I was to find that he could do more surprising things still.

Where that cab went to I have no idea. We drove to the Place Abbas, and on to the Battery, struck back along the Rue de l' Arsenal to the Greek church, twisted around a few streets, and finally came into the Arab quarter at a sharp trot. Any pursuers must have been lost by the time we drew up at a low, dirty little house behind the mosque. An Arab beckoned me from the doorway, and no sooner had I stepped out than the cab whirled away. The next instant I was inside the place and the door was slammed and barred behind me.

I found myself in absolute darkness, but the Arab took me by the hand and guided me through the gloom, and I followed in blind faith. We emerged into a large, well-lighted room, simply furnished and occupied by three men.

One was John Solomon. He lay on a cot, and greeted me with a cry of joy and a hearty handgrip. The other two were natives.

Solomon looked pretty white, and, as I dropped into a chair beside him, he hastily laid bare his shoulder. "Look at this 'ere, Doctor Firth."

He had a nasty cut below the arm, not a dangerous wound, but in bad condition. Fortunately, I had some lint in my bag, and, sending the natives for water, I soon had the wound washed and dressed.

"You're all right," I said, relieved. "Now, let's have a chin-chin. Where did you get that memento?"

"Malta," he returned, leaning back on his pillows. "It's a werry bad thing, sir, when it comes to me a-getting cut up, it is that. Where's me mail?"

I gave it to him, and while he went over it, I inspected the two natives. Both sat on mats, watching. One was an eagle-faced Arab clad in a remarkable burnoose of pure white wool, and the other man was an *askari*—a Sudanese in uniform, with the eagle of the United States consulate on his collar.

"Werry good," and Solomon looked up with a sigh of relief. "Now, Doctor Firth, how soon can I travel?"

"Right away, with care," I replied. "Look here, John Solomon, what the dickens is going on, anyhow? By the way, I've seen some more of your beads—" And I told him about Molly Quaintance. He showed no surprise, only nodding sadly.

"Yes, sir. I would 'ave met 'er at Malta, only for this 'ere nasty cut."

"You—*what?*" I stared at him, utterly astounded. Was there anything in the world that this amazing man did not know? He merely nodded again, enjoying my discomfiture.

"Yes, sir, just that. I know 'er uncle, but not 'er; 'im and me is in on this 'ere deal as partners, so to speak. Werry fine man 'e is, Doctor Firth. Yes, that 'ere Parrish 'as won every 'and so far, dang it! 'E's been an' knocked me out, 'e's got clear away from me men, and 'e's got a mortal lot o' them beads—"

"What are those beads, for the love of Heaven?" I pleaded.

John looked solemnly at me, then grinned—if his grimace could be called a grin.

"It'll keep, sir, but this 'ere gentleman won't." With which he glanced at the handsome Arab who rose and swept to the couch at my side. He was a very stately man.

"Take this packet safe to the emir," and Solomon handed him a small package, speaking the while in Arabic. "Tell him that the Turks and the Senussiyeh are against me, that I am wounded and with but one friend, and that if he does not meet me with aid at Taima I am lost."

The stately Arab bowed slightly.

"The dogs of the Senussiyeh do not hunt in the country of Nejd," he answered, and flashed a smiling glance at me. "First the friend, then the road, as the Prophet said: you have chosen a man of steel in this infidel, O Suleiman! Salaam."

He turned and strode from the room. Solomon chuckled.

"The beggar didn't know as how you spoke Arbi, sir! Well, 'e liked you, so that is one werry good thing, says I."

I grunted. "What do you care whether he liked me or not? I must say you took a strange way of appealing to the emir, whoever he is, John! Why not bluff him!"

"You don't know them Arabs, sir. This 'ere man as was just 'ere, 'e ain't o' much account in Port Said. But in Nejd, on the inside so to speak, 'e's a mortal big man, Doctor Firth. You wait—just like that, sir. You wait."

I shut up, though I was highly excited, while Solomon chattered with the *askari* from the consulate in some strange tongue akin to Arabic. Nejd, eh? Of course I knew a certain amount about that strange empire in northern Arabia, as does everyone, but the thought of going there struck fire from my imagination at once.

Nejd, whose emir is independent of anyone on earth, is pure Arabian. In ancient times it was Christian, as was the whole of Arabia and Persia; after the rise of Islam all Christianity vanished, and in Nejd the old Arabian stock is to-day at its purest and best. There are all kinds of myths about the place, naturally, and I knew very little; yet I could imagine that Solomon had flung himself upon the hospitality and aid of the emir, though I did not know that he and the emir were ancient friends and sworn brothers.

Well, Solomon finished with the *askari*, who drew himself up and saluted, then went to the door and disappeared. With that, Solomon drew out his clay pipe, whittled it full of his vile tobacco, lighted it, and lay back again with another sigh.

"Now, Doctor Firth, let's 'ave a bit o' talk. 'And me that 'ere coat, if you'll be so kind, sir."

I handed him his coat, which lay on the floor beside his couch, and he dug into a pocket painfully. Then he drew out his collection of beads, and I settled down with keen interest for the explanation. It was long in coming, however.

First, he passed me the beads and asked what I could make of them. This was little enough. All were very beautiful, some were chipped and worn: the best I could say was that since the Arabic characters had no vowel points, the beads must have been made close to the time of Muhammad himself. Arabic vowel-points were not invented until later, and then only that the Koran might be interpreted exactly. Solomon nodded eagerly at me.

"Werry good, sir. They was made quite a bit after Muhammad died, howsoever. Now, sir, if you'll be so good as to 'and me that Koran on the shelf I'll read you a bit o' werry interesting stuff."

I gave him the Koran, which was an Arabic copy, and he proceeded to read me the Sura of the Elephant. I knew the story, of course. Shortly before Muhammad's birth, in the year 568, King Abraha of Sana had moved on Mecca to destroy the last visages of heathenism in Arabia, for at that period the whole country was Christian. Abraha had been shattered and destroyed.

The rise of Islam had completed the ruin of the Christian Church in Arabia, only the triumphant Sura of the Elephant leaving to future generations a memory of what that church had once been. I had seen the ruins of Abraha's cathedral at Sana, which had been extensively studied by Eli Graves, and I wondered what connection the beads had with all this ancient history. I found that Solomon was not to be hurried, however.

"Now, sir, if you'll be a-lookin' at this 'ere map," and John took from the leaves of the Koran a folded paper, which I found to be a map of Arabia, "that there triangle is me point, sir."

Upon the map was drawn a triangle in red ink. The lines ran from Harrara in Oman to El Harik in Nejd, thence to Marib in Yemen, and back to Harrara—each leg measuring some five hundred miles, the base eight hundred. I knew what the place was, and said so. On Arab maps and charts it is called Roba el Khali, or the Abode of Emptiness. Even to the Arabs it is totally unknown and unexplored, and they say that in the centre is a place called El Ahkaf—an enormous quicksand able to engulf whole caravans.

Well, I looked at the map, and there sure enough was El Ahkaf marked in red ink as an irregular area, having a cross in the centre. Also, there were other places marked within that triangle. In the north the Tamarisk Mountains, or Jeb el Athar; in the centre the Flower Country, or Belad es Zohur, just fringing the quicksands.

"We made this 'ere map nigh on ten year ago," observed Solomon reflectively.

"Who did?" I asked, looking up at him. "Were you ever in that country?"

"Yes, sir. Me an' Mr. Graves made the map, we did that. It was 'im as first got some o' them 'ere beads, Doctor Firth. The same ones as the young lady 'as now. Some werry queer things we found in that there country, sir, some things as you wouldn't believe on if I told you. It was there that the last of the Christian Arabs went, after Muhammad 'ad cleared the rest of Arabia."

He spoke quite simply, as if he were merely telling me about the weather. Yet that triangle was absolutely unknown to the world. Palgrave had never crossed it, and Doughty had died with the feat in mind; even the Arabs shunned it like a country cursed of Allah. Graves had never written of it in his books, and to hear this fat little Cockney calmly declare that he had himself mapped it out was a staggering thing. But I believed him.

"What has all this got to do with the beads?" I asked slowly, "and with the Emir of Neid? You told his messenger to meet you at Taima, which is a city in from the coast above Mecca and—"

"Eighty mile in, sir," nodded John, his blue eyes twinkling a little. "Mr. Graves is at Aden. If so be as we get to Taima, the emir 'e'll meet us and we'll all meet wi' Mr. Graves at them there Tamarisk Mountains. This 'ere is a big thing, Doctor Firth, just like that."

"But what about the beads?" I persisted, irritated. "What are the blasted things, John? I'm blessed if I can see what you're driving at!"

"Well, sir, I'd werry much prefer not to tell you just yet, not even 'ere in the 'ouse o' my friends," he returned, looking down at the beads which I had given back to him. "You wait, sir, till so be as we're out on the desert. It's safer. I don't feel just right in me mind, Doctor Firth, about that there man Parrish. I can't get 'im out o' me 'ead, as the cook said about the new butler."

Solomon ceased abruptly, and his wide blue eyes went from me to the doorway. I caught a faint sound from somewhere without, and John rose in bed and put one hand to the bare wall at his back. I paid no attention to his movement, but stared down at the map and wondered anew at the mystery of this man and his place in the world.

Then, very suddenly, came a horrible strangled cry from the outer rooms. I leaped up in alarm; as I did so, a revolver crashed out with deafening report, close at hand. The acrid reek of the smoke blinded me, and the powder burned my face, so close was it. The room was filled with smoke and noises, and before I could move something crashed into me and sent me to the floor.

A weight of men fell upon me, knocking out my breath, and I felt my arms bound in a twinkling. The suddenness of the whole affair dazed and bewildered me, gave me not the slightest notion of what was happening. Then the men piled off me and I was jerked up; as the dense smoke cleared off, I looked around for Solomon. He had vanished completely from the room in that brief instant!

With that, I perceived why. He had doubtless reached out his hand to some hidden spring, and rolled from the couch into a concealed passage of some sort. For half a dozen Arabs were searching furiously, pounding walls and floor, while in front of me stood Lionel Parrish, his terrible brown eyes searching my face.

"So," and his cold, bell-like voice vibrated ominously, "we missed the fox and caught the jackal, eh? How do you do, Doctor Firth? I trust you remember me."

CHAPTER IV

I TAKE A JOURNEY

THERE WAS nothing half-way about the villainy of
Lionel Parrish. As I stood before him in that bare room
whence Solomon had vanished, as I gazed into those cold brown
eyes, where a devil lurked, as I noted anew the finely chiselled
features and regal manner of him, I felt exactly as I had felt in
the chart-house of the liner. He was not a man, but a thing.

I thought then, and I have thought ever since, that Parrish
was absolutely sincere in all he did. He was working for the
Senussiyeh, for Islam, and it dehumanized him utterly. I never
remember having seen a smile or twinkle of mirth on his face
and when he did smile, there was anything but mirth in his
eyes. He was a machine driven by sheer will-power, a monstrous
distortion in spirit of the best-shapen man who ever walked the
earth and drew its homage.

Solomon expressed it exactly when he said, entirely without
blasphemy: "God made 'im, and was so scared o' what 'E'd been
an' done that 'E broke the mould. And thank God for it, says I!"

Parrish stood looking at me for a long moment, and it
required all my control to meet that satanic gaze and not falter.
But I did it, partly because I was slowly growing angry and partly
because I was so desperately frightened that I was ashamed to
let him see it. A little flicker of admiration stole into his brown
eyes. There was a hypnotic power in him, increased by that odd
forked beard, which came near to mastering me.

"Well, Doctor Firth," he said quietly, motioning his men to

abstain from their vain search, "I imagine there is very little use in our beating around the bush. You know who I am, of course?"

"I wish I didn't," was my answer. "Otherwise, I would have admired you. But one can't well admire a dog in a lion's skin."

The shot at his pride went home. His thin nostrils quivered, and with something very like horror I saw his forked beard twist and writhe a little, as though made of snakes. But the man was vibrant with electricity.

"You compliment me," he said, and his eyes brought out the sweat on my brow. "But it is a little early in the game for compliments, doctor." He stooped and picked up the map which I had dropped in the struggle. A glance at it, and he thrust it into his pocket. Then he drew out something that glittered in the light, and his lips curved into a smile as he watched me.

For I recognized the silver chain and the beads instantly. Where had he got hold of them? I myself had seen Molly Quaintance hand them over to the purser!

"So your eyes widen, eh?" and there was a bitter mockery in his voice. "Your friend left the ship at Suez, doctor, and is at present a guest on my yacht there. Her future depends largely upon yourself."

I did not hurl the lie at him, as a proper hero should. The thing had horrified me far past any melodrama, because I saw that he spoke the truth. Molly Quaintance was in his hands, and those cursed beads had something to do with it all! I could only stare at him and wait for him to continue.

"From this map, from your intimacy with my friend Solomon, and from various other indications, Doctor Firth, I believe you know a good deal too much for your health. It would be very easy to kill you, but I prefer to make use of you. Let me inform you that instead of meeting Professor Graves at Aden, Miss Quaintance and I will meet him at Marib, in Yemen. I have already informed him of that fact. Now, whether she meets him in her present untouched condition or not depends largely on you."

"How?" I asked thickly, wondering if I was in some horrible nightmare.

"In two ways. First, you are a physician, and I will have need of your services. Second, I want information from you—all you know. Give me your parole, and Miss Quaintance shall not be harmed, nor shall you."

A curious change seemed to come over me in that moment, and it is very hard to explain. Until I left the hotel that morning I had been like any other decent American citizen—with a firm faith in my own civilization, living in a world of the twentieth century, smoking British cigars, and reading by electric light. Now all that was swept away. I was plunged into a maelstrom of the dark ages dependent on my own brain and sinew. I was thrust from a battle of competition into a competition of battle; the absurdity of my situation was changed to a horrible reality, and I accepted it almost unconsciously, and faced it squarely then and afterward.

"How can I trust you?" I asked, and perhaps impelled by some volition of that man's devilish brain, I put the question in Arabic. He seemed not surprised.

"These men are *khuan* or brethren of the order," and his eyes swept to the men who bowed slightly in deference. "They will witness my oath upon the Koran and by Allah, that my promises be kept."

Strange though it may seem, I did not doubt him; I could not doubt him. There was deadly sincerity in his voice—the horrible sincerity of a thing, not of a man. I knew that he took the oath with the same dispassionate coldness in which he would have killed me had he wished.

Had it been for my own sake only, I honestly think I would have braved it out and stood by Solomon. There was Molly Quaintance to be considered, however, and all the beads and maps in the world would not compensate for any harm done her.

"I accept," I returned simply. He nodded, as a matter of course.

"Very well. Do you know where Solomon went?"

"No."

"A secret passage, probably. No matter. Did he make this map?"

"Yes."

"When?"

"Ten years ago, he said."

"How many of the hundred beads has he?"

"I do not know—perhaps sixty or less." So there were a hundred beads, then! My answer drew a little breath like a sigh from the men around, and Parrish's eyes flashed.

"Do you know what those beads refer to?"

"No."

That negative relieved the tension unmistakably, I was glad to see. Parrish looked at me for a moment thoughtfully.

"You were to accompany Solomon, without knowing of the quest?"

"He was just about to tell me when you interrupted."

"Very well. Then I have your parole?"

"As far as Marib," I returned, though without any definite reason for the answer save a desire not to bind myself to this man indefinitely. A satirical smile flitted into his cruel face, and he said something to the Arabs in a tongue I did not understand. Then he nodded to me.

"Very good, doctor. After Marib I rather think your safest course will be to stick to me, as you may see for yourself. Now, you had best get into these clothes."

One of the Arabs brought in two outfits of desert dress complete to the last detail, and Parrish showed me how to get into the things, which smelled vilely of camels. First came the *kamis*, or white cotton shirt, from neck to ankles, and over it he threw a really magnificent cloak of pure white wool lined with silk, which fastened by elaborate gold-twisted cords. A crimson sash around my waist, a crooked dagger stuck through it, a pair of slippers of red leather, and I was nearly dressed.

Parrish said something to one of his men, who produced a bottle of stain which was applied to my feet, legs, face, and hands, until I was brown as a berry. Now came a white skullcap, over which was thrown a large crimson silk kerchief, bound by a fillet of wool, and I was complete, if somewhat awkward. The Arabs passed no jests upon my looks, however; they were men of a deadly seriousness, and if they were really brethren of the Senussiyeh, I began to perceive that I was extremely lucky to escape with my life.

One of them picked up my instrument-case, while Parrish quickly donned his own costume. When he was through, he was as much an Arab as any of the rest, though his dress and mine were far finer than those of the others.

"Come," he said simply, and we left the place behind.

As we left the little doorway, I caught sight of a huddled body lying inside the door, and knew it for that of the Arab who had admitted me. Parrish must have made his raid sharply and surely, for Solomon had had no warning. Walking to the Rue Quai du Nord, we took a tramcar direct to the water front.

I could not but admire the fashion in which Parrish trusted to my word, when a cry to any of the passing constables would have gained me freedom. But all the boasted might of civilization was powerless to save Molly Quaintance, and there was a wild thrill of eagerness coursing through my veins. Neither she nor I seemed in any pressing danger; more, I was bound for Arabia, it appeared. If Parrish had spoken truth, we were going to Marib, directly inland from Hodeidah, and I would see a country which few white men have ever seen. Whatever those beads were, there was undoubtedly a big venture afoot, and a desperate one.

Drawn up against the quay on the Rue Sultan Osman was a large motor-launch, her awnings out. We went directly to her, three Arab seamen appeared and saluted Parrish, and we piled in at once. Just as the lines were being cast off, I saw an odd thing.

Sauntering idly along the quay above us was an *askari* from

the United States consulate—the same black man I had seen
in Solomon's room! I looked up at him and met his eyes, but if
he recognized me he made no sign; then our motor started up,
and we swept out into the Ismail Basin. The sight of that *askari*
was inexpressibly cheering, however; he was no fool, or he would
not be associated with John Solomon, I told myself. Wherein I
was quite right, for once.

Port Said soon lay behind us as we darted down Lake Menza-
leh. It was only a little after one o'clock, and I was pleasurably
surprised to see Parrish beckon me to the after deck, where a
table was being set out beneath the awning. One of the Arabs
was sitting beside Parrish, and as I approached he rose with a
bow.

"Doctor Firth, this is Sidi Akhbar ibn Zalib," said Parrish,
in English.

To my surprise, Sidi Akhbar proved to be a graduate of
Harvard and Oxford, and the three of us enjoyed a delight-
ful meal. It was hard for me to realize that I sat with enemies,
one an Arab and the other a renegade. Parrish himself betrayed
a mind of amazing power; Sidi Akhbar was a brother of the
Senussiyeh, a thin-lipped man of middle age and very gloomy
eyes, but pleasant enough.

I learned several things which surprised me for both men
spoke freely to a certain extent about their huge monastic
order. It seemed that they sent their younger members to all
the universities in Europe and America; that the grand lodge,
located somewhere in the Sahara, maintained great factories and
depots of all descriptions; and that they were successfully holding the Italians to a strip of the Libyan coast. Nor was this any
idle talk, for I later confirmed it in every particular, and found
it well known to the British in Egypt, where the Senussiyeh is
the bugbear of all men.

Only once did Parrish make any reference to the real situation. We were darting past a huge German liner, and I was just

lighting my cigar, the others not smoking, when Parrish gave me a single look.

"Please remember, doctor, that your parole includes an abstinence from all discussion with Miss Quaintance. I am quite frank in saying that I wish neither you nor her to learn the object of this expedition, at least for the present. I will, of course, trust to your honour in this matter."

Before I could reply, Sidi Akhbar showed his calibre. Leaning forward with a sharp ejaculation, he spoke in entire disregard of my feelings, using Parrish's Moslem name:

"Sidi Abu Talib, this is too important to trust in the honour of any infidel! By Allah, it were better—"

Parrish gave him a slow glance of such utter venomous anger that the Arab drew back, with a shifty pallor stealing into his features.

"Who is master here, you or I? What I have said, I have said. Do you agree, Doctor Firth?"

Naturally, I agreed. There was nothing else to be done but to agree. After I had done so, every thing became very pleasant once more.

One thing, however, I noticed both in Sidi Akhbar and those other brethren of the order who were on the launch— and I noticed it later in all the rest of Parrish's men. They never smiled. They seemed driven by some compelling purpose which rendered them anxious-eyed, intent, and tense, as though the outcome of the world hung upon the result of their mission.

And to a certain extent, that was exactly the case. As I said at the outset of this story, there are terrible and incredible things to be related if I am to do justice to the memory of John Solomon. Those who have lived in the East will know if I speak the truth; others may believe me or not, as they please.

We reeled off the kilometres in fine style that afternoon; our craft was too small to be subject to traffic regulations or, perhaps. Parrish was too big a man to be detained. At all events we reached Suez shortly after seven o'clock that evening, and went straight to the yacht of which Parrish had already made mention.

She was not a pretty yacht, being a slovenly grey in hue and very poorly cared for, but she was a large craft, and had good lines. Parrish had sent some cables from Ismailia, so that we found her with anchor out of the mud and steam up; barely had our launch tender been taken in tow when her engine began to turn, and we started past Port Ibrahim.

Parrish was her absolute master beyond question. Men saluted him right and left, though their only uniformity of costume seemed to be a brown burnoose. Sidi Akhbar took me to a small stateroom aft, and requested me to appear in the dining saloon in ten minutes for dinner.

That suited me well enough, and I found the saloon by the help of an Arab seaman who stuck close to my elbow. I was still wearing my flowing robes, which were not half so uncomfortable as at first. In the saloon were Parrish, Sidi Akhbar, and three other brethren of the order—all very polite, speaking cultured French or English, never smiling. A moment after I entered, Molly Quaintance appeared.

To my utter amazement, she was smiling, eager, and seemed delighted with everything; when she recognized me it was with a ripple of laughter at my disguise and a hearty handshake. She was absolutely in no more distress than if she was on the yacht of a friend! It was staggering, for a bit, until I vaguely began to perceive the reason.

She greeted Colonel Parrish with a frank handgrip and a smile, expressed herself as delighted with the yacht, and settled down at the table with an unalloyed eagerness and efficiency, which I believe rather astonished Parrish. For a girl—or woman, since she was twenty two—Molly Quaintance was certainly self-possessed and capable.

Parrish gravely informed her that I was to accompany them on "the expedition," and while I asked no questions, it was not hard to gather hints from the ensuing conversation. She knew

nothing of her destination; Parrish stated that we would meet
Professor Graves at Marib, and asked me rather pointedly to
look after Molly's comfort; and it seemed that she was a trifle
disappointed that he was not going to attend to that himself.

The whole crowd treated her with absolute deference, yet
in an odd manner hard to explain. Plainly they were picked
men, all four of them. Sidi Akhbar was a sunken-eyed fanatic,
as he proved in truth later on, yet all were gentlemen for the
time being. They had none of the Oriental sensuality in their
faces, which I think was due to the severe monastic training of
the Senussiyeh; Akhbar was an engineer; the other three were
specialists at anything from archaeology to machinery. They had
had a fifth *khuan,* an M.D. from the Royal College at London,
but he had been detained at the last moment. From what I gathered, I found that he was the pock-marked Arab Solomon had
landed safely in jail.

After dinner, Molly and I went up to the afterdeck, for it was
frightfully hot, and stretched out comfortably in Singapore
chairs, alone and unguarded. I was sorely tempted to break my
word—and for the second time by Molly herself. But I held
firm, because Parrish trusted me. My admiration for the man
was very much alive; we were both thoroughly in his power,
and, like anyone else, I was quite blind as to the future. So when
Molly told me the change in her plans, I naturally kept quiet.

Parrish, having left the liner at Alexandria, boarded it again
at Suez and took off Molly. He represented himself as a friend
of her uncle's, had letters from Professor Graves, in Aden, telling her to accompany Parrish to Marib, where he would meet
them; also, another note from the archaeologist requested Molly
to hand over the necklace to Parrish for safe-keeping. She had
no cause for any suspicion.

"Well," I said reflectively, watching the lights of a dread-
nought sweep past us through the night, "if we land at Hodeidah
and start up-country, it's a cinch that you'll have to don Arab
dress, Molly. That's why I've done it."

"Why didn't you tell me on the P. & O. boat that you were going to meet my uncle?" she demanded quickly, her violet eyes dark under the electric light. "Do you know where this expedition is going?"

"No," I laughed easily. "And as for telling you before, I was only enlisted at Port Said. However, I'm mighty glad that we're going to be in company, Miss Quaintance!"

So I gave her no warning; it would have served no good end, and would have merely made her unhappy. Besides, I doubted if Parrish intended her harm, in any fashion; that is saying a good deal, considering that he was a renegade, and his men Arabs— who say truly of themselves that "Allah gave to the Arabs nine-tenths of passion, and to the rest of the world the remainder." Yet serves to show my point that, while I knew Parrish for a bad egg, I also recognized him as working for something far above any personal ends. Men can serve the devil in absolute sincerity, as history has shown many a time.

As I retired to bed that night, however, pondering the happenings of that eventful day, it occurred to me that Parrish was very swift and terrible in all he did. Between Gibraltar and Suez he had checked Solomon, outwitted him, and had forged the letters to Molly Quaintance from her uncle. I began to realize dimly the satanic cleverness of Colonel Lionel Parrish, yet only dimly so far, for it had not fully developed. And whether John Solomon could checkmate him or not was extremely doubtful.

In fact, I decided that Solomon had been entirely eliminated as a factor.

CHAPTER V

HOW ELI GRAVES DIED

OUR TRIP to Hodeidah, and thence overland to Marib,
was short and swift, and deserves a volume to itself. At
Hodeidah our caravan was made up—forty men, with the finest
black camels in Yemen, and the men were Senussiyeh to the last
one. But the camels numbered something like two hundred,
for Parrish carried an enormous amount of luggage; and this
luggage drew a great deal of attention from him and his aides.

The more that things developed, however, the less connection could I see. What had those odd square beads to do with
the Sura of the Elephant? What had the Emir of Nejd to do
with the Abode of Emptiness? As for Solomon, he and the emir
were a thousand miles away, at Taima in the north. I had not the
vaguest notion of what it was all about, except that there were
a hundred beads involved. That meant nothing. Every Moslem
rosary contains a hundred beads, one for each of the names of
Allah.

Parrish had thirty-five or thirty-six beads, I was not sure
which. While we were encamped at noon, with Marib in the
distance, and the mountains to our left, I accidentally came upon
him counting and studying the beads; there was no mistaking
them, and I made a rough count. Also, he had removed Molly's
beads from their silver chain. I moved off, saying nothing, but
keeping rather thoughtful.

Our trip was through the mountains to Sana—an uphill
road and difficult. Molly adopted no disguise, and although we

were halted outside Sana by the Turkish troops, the influence of Parrish seemed to open everything to us. Indeed, the brethren of the Senussiyeh stalked among the Turks and Arabs with a disdainful arrogance. At Sana we made no halt, though I bribed one of the natives to show me the ruins of the cathedral built by the Christian King Abraha: and with the next morning went on to Marib, through better country.

It was a five days' trip, all told, even though our camels were not ordinary animals, but racers. At the end of it, I was absolutely down and out. Anyone who has never ridden a camel in his life cannot do five days of hard riding without suffering for it, and suffering heavily. I saw nothing of Molly Quaintance; but when we had camped outside Marib, a kindly camel man gave me some ointment, which took out the stiffness to some extent.

For three days we were camped there outside town, but nothing happened. Marib was beyond Turkish jurisdiction, and Parrish's men maintained a military camp, being well armed with Mannlichers. Molly and I were restricted to the camp limits, and since we had taken possession of a palm grove on the river above the city, it was pleasant enough.

Molly, naturally, was filled with delight over everything she saw, and I did not attempt to render her unquiet. It was all strange to me as well, but I was gradually sifting down into adjustment with my new environment, and I was worried. Parrish kept to his tent during the first two days, receiving there a steady stream of visitors. These ranged from sheikhs to beggars, and, knowing what I did of Parrish, I began to imagine that he had something more afoot than a mere trip into the unexplored regions.

With the third evening several things happened. Parrish joined us at dinner with the information that Professor Graves would arrive the next day; and immediately after dinner he carried me off to attend one of the Senussiyeh, who had a stab in the thigh. The man's name was Kasim, and his wound was slight; while I was binding it up, Parrish was called away, and we were alone in the tent. Instantly Kasim gripped my wrist.

"Firth Effendi!" he whispered rapidly. "Be quiet and listen!"

He spoke in French, and after my first involuntary start I looked down at his eager black eyes and nodded.

"Speak! I am listening."

"Effendi, my master Solomon got word to me at Sana. Be ready to fly with me, after the caravan has set forth, for if we remain with Abu Talib we are lost. We—"

At that instant another of the brotherhood entered, and Kasim fell silent. I bound up his thigh with trembling fingers, and hastened out into the open air. Stumbling across the enclosure to another tent, I sank down behind it in the warm sand, and reflected. I was more startled than I cared to admit.

And who would not have been astounded? Solomon had spies even among the *khuan* of the Senussiyeh, it appeared! Wounded, surprised, outwitted as he had been, John Solomon had yet managed to keep track of me; it was the more wonderful, because our trip had been an exceedingly rapid one. I began to feel uncomfortably like a shuttlecock knocked about between the battledores of Solomon and Parrish.

Suddenly, almost in answer to my thought, came a voice from the tent at my back. It was the voice of Sidi Akhbar, and he was addressing Parrish.

"O *mokaddem*, beloved of Allah, the report is in! The accursed infidel arrives in the morning; our men could not steal his papers, but his instruments are ruined. He is in our power. Also, here is the messenger from the Shereef of Mecca and Medina, on whom be the blessings of God!"

"Salaam!" exclaimed the cold voice of Parrish. "Speak!"

"O *mokaddem*," returned a third voice, that of the messenger, "the holy shereef, guardian of Islam, sends you this reply. If the beads of Muhammad do not lie, then will the grand master of the Senussiyeh be acknowledged as the head of Islam, and the Turks will be expelled from the land. But further, you must return with full proof that you possess the thing which you seek, and this thing must first be delivered to the holy shereef. And this message is given in the name of the Prophet, and sworn to upon the book of books."

"Good!" cried out Parrish, a savage ring of exultation in his tone. "Depart!"

I heard a shuffle of footsteps in the sand and stared up at the stars in a wild mingling of fear and astounded wonder. What secret had I thus stumbled upon by sheer accident? The danger of my position never occurred to me.

"He admits it, lord!" said the voice of Sidi Akhbar, in slow awe as if he spoke of a thing he himself had only half-believed. "He admits it, then! We seek truly!"

"Of course, fool! Now be silent!" retorted Parrish. His clear, bell-like voice rang vibrantly, and he seemed in the grip of some tremendous emotion. "Send back a messenger to our father Senussi at once, telling of this word from the shereef of the holy cities. The game is now in our hands. Before daybreak do you and the rest take out the machines to the desert beyond the city—twenty miles to the northeast. Leave ten men here with me. Set up all the machines and prepare all else, for we must make a swift journey."

As Sidi Akhbar murmured some reply, I rose and stole away softly. Remain longer I dared not, for were I discovered my fate would be certain and terrible. I knew now that Parrish was holding some terrifically big cards—and what they were mattered not. He was dealing with the Shereef of Mecca—a greater man in Arabia than the vali of the sultan, for in the shereef's hands were the two holy cities of the whole world of Islam. If he ordered it, the Turks would be expelled from Arabia at a blow; and that was exactly what Parrish had in view. When the Senussiyeh took over the holy cities of Mecca and Medina, the power of Turkey would be absolutely crushed in the East, and a new menace to Christendom would be risen, full-fledged.

Realizing all this, I was horribly afraid, and am not ashamed to admit it. All that night I lay in my tent and cursed the fate that had drawn me between the millstones of Islam; any average American would have been only too anxious to let these brown devils fight out their quarrels, I think. Yet that was not where all my fear lay.

There was something tremendous behind it which I did not know; Parrish was to bring back some mysterious "thing" which would have power to change half the world. I did not know what the machines were which he mentioned, nor where the "beads of Muhammad" came in. I could not see what my duty as a Christian gentleman was, nor why Solomon was straining every energy to whip Parrish, or why Professor Eli Graves was mixed in it. I did see, however, that if the Senussiyeh took over the holy cities, the emirate of Nejd would be seriously menaced, which explained why Solomon depended on the emir to join him. Aside from this, the whole affair was a jumble of grand masters, emirs, sultans, and Cockneys, and at last I dozed off to dream wild dreams until dawn.

Did not my story lie farther afield, I would like to spend more details upon Eli Graves, for he was a great man. He came into camp about ten in the morning, with two camels and half a dozen men. Sidi Akhbar and most of our force had departed with the caravan. Molly and I went out to meet Graves, Parrish awaiting us in his tent. Everything seemed right, at the first, and the explorer evidently had no misgivings.

He was in Arab dress, and looked a patriarch, every inch of him. He was swarthily bronzed, had powerful blue eyes and a long white beard, was very muscular for his age, and was self-contained and rather silent. Molly greeted him in wild delight, and he seemed deeply moved at meeting her; then she introduced me, and I gripped the old man's hand to find it like iron; and his blue eyes were like gimlets.

"I am pleased to meet you, sir," he said courteously. "Molly, kindly explain why you cabled me to meet you here?"

I waited for the blow to fall, and it came swiftly.

"But I did not!" cried the girl, her violet eyes wide in wonder. "You wrote me yourself to join Colonel Parrish at Suez, and to give him that chain of beads! See, here are the letters—" And she drew them from the bosom of her dress, handing them to him.

The old man turned away from us as he looked over them. I knew my guess had been correct; they were forged beyond a doubt. Yet Graves took the blow like the man he was. He must have seen that the girl suspected nothing. Thrusting the letters beneath his sash, he raised his head and looked at his camels. Four of Parrish's armed men were quietly standing beside them, rifles in hand. Graves turned to me, his face wakened to a horrible suspicion, deep lines suddenly graven about his eyes.

"What do you know of this—" he began, but I broke in impulsively.

"I'm in the same boat, Professor Graves," I said, feeling a great pity for him. "I am a prisoner like yourself, to all intents. Colonel Parrish is waiting for us yonder."

"Do you know John Solomon?" he shot out, in his deep voice, while his eyes dwelt on my face searchingly. Molly watched us in wonder.

"Yes," I nodded gravely. "Parish has outwitted him so far, but one of his men is with us."

"Then all is not yet lost," said Graves slowly, and put out his hand once more to mine. "Doctor Firth, I believe you. Let us meet this man Parrish and know the worst."

Poor Molly broke out in questioning but he motioned her to be silent, and we walked back to the tent of Parrish. That terrible inhuman man was sitting quietly, his brown face immobile, six armed men ranged about his tent. As we entered, he motioned them to leave, and his brown eyes went to the face of Graves.

"Professor Graves?" he said, with a faint sneer in his voice. "I am glad to see you. I trust you find your niece quite well?"

The explorer gazed at him, but his blue eyes were awful to look upon. Never for an instant did he lose his dignity.

"What does this mean, Colonel Parrish?"

Then, for the first and only time in my life, did I hear Parrish really laugh. It was a demoniacal laugh, harsh and keen as a sword-swish in the air; his words that followed struck like a blow, and I saw Graves go deadly pale under his tan.

"It means, Professor Graves, that you have walked into the trap." Parrish paid no heed to Molly, nor did I, though I found her hand suddenly upon my arm, where it remained. "I know the whole secret of what you have discovered in the Abode of Emptiness. I have thirty-six of the beads of Muhammad. I have an expedition waiting to cross the desert. Miss Quaintance, there, is absolutely in my power—and to save her you must talk freely. Is that clear?"

Graves stood very quiet. His fingers, resting in his sash, were trembling, and he seemed stricken with age, but his voice came deep and powerful as ever:

"Who are you, Colonel Parrish?"

"Who?" Parrish looked at him with a devilish flame in his brown eyes. "I represent the Senussiyeh, sir, and I am a Moslem. Is that answer enough?"

It was. Graves swayed where he stood. With a hideous sense of hopelessness, I saw the blood sweep into his face and ebb out again. His eyes, which had been riveted on Parrish, lifted to my face and that of the girl, and they were appalling. Molly's fingers clenched on my arm. Twice Graves tried to speak, and twice the voice failed within him, until at length he got out one hoarse whisper.

"What—what do you want—devil—"

I think we were all somewhat hypnotized by the visage of Parrish, who came to his feet and stood there watching Graves. His face was handsome, venomous, satanic in its exultation and arrogance.

"What do I want?" he cried out. "I want *all!* You fool, who are you to cope with Islam? Listen! There are six men in the world who know this secret—you and I, John Solomon, the shereef of the holy cities, the grand master of the Senussiyeh, and one of my men here."

Parrish paid no attention to me, but after a moment continued vehemently:

"In the eighth century the body of the Prophet was stolen from Medina by the sect of the accursed Shiahs, and was conveyed across the desert to the Abode of Emptiness. Since then all men have believed that the body still lay at Medina in the mosque of the Prophet; the shereefs of the holy cities have known that it was gone, but the secret has been well kept. Then, a few years ago, some of those beads turned up."

Graves seemed to awaken suddenly. Lifting his patriarchal head, he gazed at the renegade a moment; then his voice thundered out in startling fashion.

"Yes, you dog!" he cried sternly. "And when the world learns the truth, your cursed religion will crumble like powder! What will all Islam say when it learns that it has been mocked for a thousand years—that its pilgrimages and gifts and vows have been made to an empty tomb, that the body of Muhammad has been in Christian hands? Think of the laugh that will sweep over Christendom when Muhammad's body is brought to New York!"

At these words—and I confess it frankly—my first impulse was to laugh; my second, to think Professor Graves gone mad. Then I knew suddenly that it was all true, though a good deal of explanation was necessary.

For the old man's words had wakened the slumbering devil in Parrish. The inhuman brown eyes had narrowed viciously, burning like coals, the only sign of life in that face of stone. Never had Parrish looked so satanically handsome, and there was a deadly venom in his cold reply, while his two-pronged beard writhed a little.

"All very good, Professor Graves. But, as it happens, the body of Muhammad will never reach New York. Kindly remember your situation. Now, here is the map you and John Solomon made some years ago—" And he held out the map which he had taken from me in that little room at Port Said.

"I am ready to bargain. Solomon has sixty-four beads. You translated them for him, and I have the rest. Sit down here and now and write me out the translation of those sixty-four beads. Accept, and I take you and Miss Quaintance with me and guarantee you both freedom when I have attained my end: I swear it on the Koran! Refuse, and your niece shall be taken to-day into the city and sold at the first bazaar. You know what *that* means. Now choose, and quickly."

Again the old man staggered under the blow, and his face flooded deep crimson. A look of terrible horror was stamped on the girl's features, but she remained silent. Then, with a deep groan, Graves dropped his head.

"I accept," he said thickly. "God forgive me, I accept!"

Parrish's face flamed with an eager light, and he drew out a fountain pen and a notebook. Without a word he pressed them into the old man's hands; Graves stared, shuddered, and slowly wrote. Then he returned the notebook, raised both hands, and a wild cry burst from him—a cry of awful agony and despair:

"God forgive me! I—I—"

He staggered, reeled, and collapsed. I caught him as he fell, and while Molly knelt over him with a choking cry, I raised his head in my arms. One glance told me all, and I looked up at Parrish with a bitter curse:

"You hound of hell! It's apoplexy but—"

"Will he die?" inquired the renegade coldly, curiously.

His voice calmed me down instantly. I rose, meeting him eye to eye.

"He'll die before night," I said, very softly, that the girl might not hear. "You'll pay for this some day, Parrish. Mind my words, you'll pay!"

The renegade's brown eyes bored into me for a moment.

"Upon my soul, Firth," he said slowly, "I feel unaccountably inclined to have you shot and done with! Well, well—attend to Graves and we'll wait to dispose of him. I'm very sorry for what's happened, very sorry. He would have been useful."

With that he strode past me out of the tent. I felt my muscles contract as he passed, and for a bare instant I was on the point of taking him by the throat and driving my curved dagger through him. My soul was white with fury inside of me. Would to Heaven that I had obeyed the impulse, even though I had been shot a moment later! But it passed, the tent flap fell, and I was left alone with a dying man and a half-hysterical girl. It was a very good thing that I had medical skill, although Graves was beyond it.

CHAPTER VI

ESCAPE

I HAD A good many links in the chain, but I could not bind them together. The destruction of the Christian power of Arabia—the territory called the Abode of Emptiness, or Roba el Khali—the beads of Muhammad—and John Solomon. The high lights stood out well enough. Muhammad's body had been stolen from Medina by the Shiah sect of Moslems—the Senussiyeh wanted it—the Emir of Neid feared the Senussiyeh and aided Solomon. The whole affair was a tangle of loose ends to me. It sounded wild and incredible and foolish.

The preparations of Colonel Lionel Parrish were anything but foolish, however, as I reflected on seeing them two days after the death of Professor Eli Graves, who had never regained consciousness. Parrish meant business, and he was going to his end with all the calm certitude of a machine. He left nothing to chance—and that was his only mistake.

Molly, stricken by grief and the realization of her danger—Parrish and I had rejoined the main caravan in the desert twenty miles outside Marib. The renegade fully intended to keep the girl in safety till his work was done; he meant to redeem the promise he had made Graves, and could do it best by taking Molly with him. I am quite willing to give the devil his due in this matter. Molly's beauty never touched him in the least, for he was absolutely inhuman, but his oath on the Koran was sacred to him.

So, with Graves buried decently, we were now ready to be off. I was agreeably disappointed in finding that camel travel

was over. The Senussiyeh was up to the minute in all it did. To
transport our entire force of forty-seven, Parrish had, set up
and ready to the last detail, five motor-driven six-wheeled sand
sledges; they were exactly of the type which the French use in the
Sahara, and would probably serve here excellently. They required
petrol, of course, and how the difficulty was to be met I did not
see until that evening, when Parrish called me into consultation
with his four aides.

"Sit down, Doctor Firth," he said coldly, when I had followed
my summoner into the tent. "Since you have gained some idea
of the purpose of this expedition, I propose to make all the use
of you I can. As you may be aware, these sledges of ours can do
about fifteen miles an hour across the loose desert sands, and
the five can easily hold all our party.

"Now," he continued, watching me steadily with those inhuman eyes, "your medicine case contains a very complete medici-
nal equipment, and I want you to give every man in our party a
thorough preventive against fevers, since we have to cross some
very low and unhealthy country. This must be done within the
next two hours."

"How about your petrol?" I inquired, nodding assent. "If you
ran short of *essence*, you're going to be in a bad way—"

"We do not intend to run short," he returned. "We must cover
some four hundred miles each way, doctor. Allowing for delays,
we will cover two hundred miles a day. Our cars are specially
built with petrol-containing bodies; each car has enough petrol
to carry it for a thousand miles. Further, a caravan leaves Marib
to-morrow with a fresh supply, and we will meet it on our return
trip. Thus there will be no failure. Now, one of the bazaars in
Marib sells British drugs imported from Damascus, and whatever you wish to order will be brought you to-night. We leave
at dawn."

I bowed slightly and left the tent. My own helplessness
dismayed me. Flight was out of the question in this country,
where an infidel was practically shot on sight, and the man Kasim

had kept out of reach. With the death of Graves, it seemed that Solomon had been utterly stricken out of all calculations, and Molly and I could only go through with the programme and trust that Parrish would keep his word in the end.

So, having plenty of quinine and nitre, and not knowing what brand of fever to guard against, I prepared a nauseous but healthy dose, mixed in plenty of cascara, and at least managed to better the rough-and-ready Arab medical practice. The Senussiyeh took it man by man, at Parrish's order, and when Kasim's turn came he grinned at me and whispered something about missing my chance to poison the whole crowd. I promptly gave him a kick that sent him sprawling; the others laughed, and so the incident passed.

After dinner that evening Molly and I wandered to the edge of the camp, which was under military guard, with sentries at intervals, and stretched out on a little hillock of sand that overlooked the desert. The girl was still grief-stricken and silent, but I did my best to relieve her despondency by telling her of Solomon; after that scene between her uncle and Parrish, I knew that of course the ban was lifted on our discussion of the expedition. While we were talking, there came a low voice from behind us:

"Effendi! Do not look around."

Just in time, I laid a restraining hand on the girl's wrist. The voice was that of Kasim, and I thrilled to it.

"I am listening," was my soft reply. Kasim continued swiftly in French:

"Effendi, I am on guard until midnight. Bring Mademoiselle Quaintance, an hour after midnight, to where the machines are set up. We must steal one and depart—"

"Mademoiselle Quaintance is in no danger," I broke in. "She cannot—"

"Effendi! For the love of Allah, trust to me!" and there was desperate entreaty in the man's voice, "ft is the order of my master. To-morrow destruction falls upon these men, and we must avoid it or perish with them. Question not, but meet me an hour after midnight; I have arms and all things needful."

"I will be there," I returned, and when I looked around Kasim had vanished.

Molly, who understood French well enough, was steadied instantly by the evident proximity of the unknown danger. It was no time for hysterics or wild questionings, and her firm sweet character was brought out to the full by the crisis. We talked over the situation calmly, and when at length she rose to return, she placed both hands in mine, and I caught the shimmer of tears in her violet eyes as she spoke, quietly and simply:

"Whatever you say, Doctor Firth, I will do. Uncle has more than once spoken to me about this Mr. Solomon, and I know he trusted him absolutely. I only wish that my presence did not cause you worry and—"

"Tut, tut!" I broke in, trying to maintain my best professional manner, but without any great success. Her slender blue-clad figure, the wavy blue-black sheen of her hair in the starlight, the clear and frank woman face—it intoxicated me, lifted me out of myself. "My dear Molly, your presence causes me only a great happiness that I can possibly be of service to you. Now let's get back to the tents; yours adjoins mine, and you can go to sleep at once. I'll waken you by midnight."

With her hand still in mine, we walked back together, and I saw her safe into her tent. I had no preparations to make, other than to get my small instrument case, and after I had left Molly I stood gazing out across the camp at the blank desert, wondering. What was this "destruction" of which Kasim spoke?

"By thunder!" I thought eagerly. "Old Solomon is still in the ring, it seems!"

Thoughtfully enough, I returned to my own tent, my respect for the pudgy Cockney vastly increased. He had some blow ready to descend on Parrish, certainly; yet it was very odd what Kasim had said about our perishing also if we remained.

"What are your initials, Doctor Firth?"

Startled, I turned. In the doorway of my low tent was standing Parrish, the gloomy-eyed Sidi Akhbar at his side. The light of my single candle struck full on the renegade's arrogant handsome features, and I read in them a quick gleam of ferocity.

"Go!" he said to the Arab, before I could speak. "I will myself attend to this."

Sidi Akhbar flashed me one malignant glance, saluted, and vanished. Parrish came into the tent and stood looking at me coldly. The tent flap had fallen behind him.

"Since my name is Walter Firth," I replied, "my initials would naturally be W.F. Why?"

"Those words seal your death warrant, sir," he answered evenly, and handed me a many-folded paper. "I cannot afford to have plotters in my ranks. That paper was taken from a man this evening, who came disguised as a beggar. Read it!"

With my brain in a turmoil of bewilderment, I opened the paper and held it to the candle. There stared up at me the fine copperplate of Solomon's writing, and this was the wording of the unsigned note:

> W.F.: Get Miss Q. away from P. at once. Nejd men are waiting for him, and have orders to slay without quarter. The man who brings you this will guide you safely.

I shall never forget the way my heart sank as I read those words. Solomon's messenger had bungled—doubtless paying for it with his life. This, then, was the destruction of which Kasim had spoken—and Parrish, fully warned, would escape it now! Once more the renegade had outwitted the Cockney.

But, as I stared down at that note, I suddenly realized what Parrish had said. My fate was sealed. A swift vivid surge of hatred swelled up within me, but it died away into terrible caution as I looked up at Parrish. The crisis had come, indeed, and my only hope lay in overpowering this devil on the spot, and getting away.

Fortunately, he knew nothing of Kasim being Solomon's man.

It lacked an hour of midnight, and if I was to save myself, all our plans must be altered. Yet there was no alternative. I stared at the renegade and allowed my inward horror to show clearly in my face, till his proud eyes tinged with contempt.

"You will die at dawn," he said, quite dispassionately. "If you have any final request to make, I will hear it now."

His cold brown eyes almost paralyzed me as I stood, but shaking off the hypnosis with a great effort, I played out my hand desperately. Knowing well that his slightest cry would give the alarm, that my slightest movement would warn him, that I must strike before he so much as imagined it, I did the only thing possible.

"Don't kill me!" I cried out, assuming a frantic horror which I was very near to feeling in reality. "You don't have to do that, Parrish—I'll promise secrecy, I'll help you—give me a chance to live—"

"Stop that babbling!" he broke in, with stern contempt. I took a step toward him, my hands clasped in pleading. "If you have any coherent request to make, say it."

Another step, and I was close beside him, pleading wide-eyed for my life in as abject a manner as I could force myself to act.

"Don't kill me!" I repeated wildly, clasping the shoulder of his burnoose as I sank partly to my knees, yet with every nerve and muscle tensed. "Only let me live, and I'll serve you—I'll follow you anywhere—even into hell, you dog!"

And with that I had him by the throat, with both hands. He was taken utterly by surprise, for I had flung myself directly up at him; his pronged board struck my chin, his snarling face grinned in ghastly fashion against mine—and crooking my leg behind him, I flung him under me to the sand.

None the less, the surprise was all that saved me, for he was a man of iron. Forgetting his weapons momentarily, he tore at my arms to loosen his throat from my grip: I freed my right hand, in deadly fear lest he draw a revolver, and whipped out the crooked dagger from my sheath. For an instant I was near running it through him, but even in my anger I could not do that; much as I feared and hated him, I only put the point to his throat, and his arms fell quiet as he stared up with bulging eyes.

"I'd like to kill you," I muttered thickly, "but that's the difference in breed, you hound. I'm going to make sure of you, however."

Reversing the dagger in my hand, and catching it by the blade, I brought down the heavy bone hilt just behind his ear. It was a sickening thing to do, yet I dared do nothing else. He groaned and writhed under the clutch of my left hand, then I brought down the weapon again, and drove the senses from him with another blow in the same spot.

But it was brutal work, and unnerved me far more than the brief struggle preceding it. I drew back from his prostrate figure, and sheathed my weapon, trembling in every limb. Despite the grim inhumanity of the renegade, despite his pitiless cruelty and heart of stone, to deliberately strike him unconscious was an awful thing. Yet the time was not far distant when I was to regret most bitterly that I had not obeyed that first impulse and driven the steel through him—aye, though it made of me a murderer!

I looked down at him and shuddered. There was no time to be lost, however, and this man was undeserving of pity or kindliness. Stooping down, I drew off his white wool cloak for Molly's use, and searched him.

That "frisking" was a happy afterthought. Not only did I get two excellent Webley service revolvers and cartridge belt, but I also found Parrish's share of the mysterious hundred beads, which I promptly pocketed. Taking a small electric flash lamp as well, I discarded a number of papers in Arabic, tied him hand and foot with his own head-cloth, blew out my candle, and left the tent cautiously.

Sidi Akhbar was close at hand, though the men were asleep in a dark clump just beyond the half-dozen tents. I put my mouth to the flap of Molly's tent and whispered her name. She must have been wide awake, for she replied instantly and appeared in person almost immediately.

"Is it midnight?" she asked quickly, taking the cloak I handed her.

"Not yet," I said grimly. "We have to light out of here in a hurry. Are you ready?"

"All ready," she said, and slipped her hand into mine with a quick grasp, which I returned as I led her toward the assembled machines on the other side of camp.

Naturally, the Senussiyeh had no thought of danger, especially from us, and if the other guards noticed us, they paid no attention. We approached the dark figure which stood near the machines, and at the first word from me it proved to be Kasim himself.

"*Tout est fait,*" I said rapidly. "The *mokaddem* intercepted a message from Solomon and came to my tent; I seized and bound him, and we must fly at once. Are the petrol and supplies aboard those machines?"

He was a quick-witted rascal, and wasted no time in questions.

"They are all ready, effendi. Come!"

Approaching the nearest of the five cars, I loaded Molly into the central seat. They were large, six-wheeled affairs, holding ten men each with ease, and ran partly by wheel and partly by sled-runners, thus insuring a good grip on the loose sand. The body and sides of the car were double, and served as petrol reservoirs in addition to the regular tank underneath; it had a light top, electric self-starter and lamps, and the Senussiyeh must have spent a pretty penny on the outfit.

Under the three transverse seats were stored skins of water, with provisions. Kasim placed his rifle in straps beneath the seats, where I saw other rifles as well, then he motioned me to get in beside the girl.

"I will run her, effendi," he whispered. "First, however, I must see to the other cars. I cannot disable them except temporarily, but that will give us a start."

I nodded and climbed in beside Molly, and the thrill of the moment set my pulses to leaping. I had overcome Parrish! That thought alone was like wine, and all memory of poor Graves was swept away from me in a wave of exultation. Where we were going I neither knew not cared, for Molly Quaintance was at my side, and her hand reposed in mine. The next instant I cursed myself for a brute; she trusted me, that was all, and I must prove worthy. The thought sobered me at once.

The night was clear dark-blue around us, starlit and beautiful. No sound of alarm rose from the camp; the moon had sunk long before, and escape loomed large before us. Then Kasim was leaning up to me like a shadow:

"Effendi! May Allah lighten the pains of hell for you! Is the *mokaddem* dead?"

"No," I said thankfully.

"Then I will see to it—"

"None of that," I exclaimed sharply, catching his shoulder. "You climb in and get out of here. You're not going to murder any helpless man, whoever he is. In with you, and quick about it—"

From somewhere behind us rose a vibrant shout, and there was no mistaking the bell-like voice. Parrish had come to his senses—and, like a fool, I had forgotten to gag him! Even as I realized the fact, other voices rose upon the night, and with no further parley Kasim sprang into the front seat of the machine.

With a whirring thrum the engine sprang into life, and we began to move. This gave the alarm, even more than the shouts of Parrish. I heard a yell, and another, then a spat of fire broke the night behind, and a bullet shrilled overhead.

A stifled cry broke from Molly—the poor girl must have been strung up to a tremendous tension. I put my arm about her shoulders, and pressed her down under shelter, while the car went lurching out into the desert. The yells became fainter in the rear, but the crackle of rifles leaped out after us.

It must have been then that Kasim was hit, though he said nothing of it, and made no sound. The bullets tore all around us, splintering the sides of the car, whistling and shrieking; one scraped the wool of my head kerchief like a finger passing across my head, but Molly was well sheltered, and I remained unhurt.

The car leaped and bounded over the sand, and two moments later we raced down a little crest and were out of sight and sound of the camp. If there was pursuit, we knew nothing of it. We kept on at the same speed for an hour, none of us speaking; then I suddenly became aware that Kasim was doing a poor job of guiding.

Leaning forward, I warned him of a gully ahead. He made no answer, and as I reached past him and turned the steering wheel, he collapsed and fell limply in the bottom of the car. In swift alarm I threw off the power and climbed across the front seat, drawing out the electric flash lamp I had taken from Parrish. One swing of the light was enough. Kasim had been shot through the neck, and had bled to death as he sat.

And ahead of us was the desert—untracked, unexplored, with death behind us.

CHAPTER VII

THE DESERT TRACK

"BUT WE'VE kept to the north-east, haven't we, Walter?"

"I'm not so sure, Molly. I rather imagine this compass is magnetically affected; Kasim, knowing it, could have made allowances, but it seems to have led us all astray. If our water holds out, we'll arrive at the Persian Gulf sooner or later, but the speedometer shows three hundred and ten miles, and this desert shows no signs of relief yet."

Molly leaned back, pale with the terrific heat. Even the slight breeze caused by our motion was like a solid wave of refracted heat. For we were in what would be called in Algeria a "shott"— a horizon-wide salt lake bottom, quaggy in places, but overlaid with white salt in all directions, burning and acrid to the nostrils.

It was the evening of the second day after our escape, and in all that time we had seen no living thing. On Kasim's body I had found a battered compass and a map very similar to that of Solomon's, except that there was a course laid directly to the north-east, with a cross at the end about where the cross had stood on Solomon's map. It looked very much to me as though we had diverged from our course, however.

Under the circumstances, naturally, my relations with Molly had assumed a certain degree of intimacy. She was not the sort of girl to be a prude in such a case, and I had sense enough to treat her exactly as I would have treated a partner of the male sex; two people with a modicum of sense can get along very well under any conditions, and Mrs. Grundy does not obtain in Arabia.

The farther we proceeded, the more I admired the perfect foresight Parrish had displayed in getting his equipment together. Then I began to realize a wonderful thing. He had said to Graves that these beads first began to turn up some years ago, and it was clear that in some way the beads were the key to the whole affair. Solomon and Graves had made their map ten years before. Since the beads began to "turn up," Parrish or the Senussiyeh must have had men at work getting an idea of this desert country, else they could never have so thoroughly provided against all contingencies. Solomon and Molly Graves had come from America to join the old explorer for his expedition; Parrish had got wind of it, and had pushed forward his preparations; thus, after years of preparatory work on either side, affairs had come to a head at the precise moment for me to step in and take up my share of the work!

Or, on the other hand, Solomon might have figured on drawing an outsider into the game. I never did really know how long he had had me under observation. At all events, I was now drawn into a fight of tremendous proportions, considering the results involved; even yet I did not know the full measure of those results. I rather looked on that talk of Muhammad's body as a myth.

As the moon was not due to rise until after midnight, we halted in the midst of the boggy salt waste to get a decent bit of sleep and proceed by moonlight. What had become of Parrish and Solomon's ambush of Nejd men, I did not know. As we halted in the sunset, Molly searched the horizon with the binoculars we found in the car, and, to our joy, we made out low hills to the north.

"We'll head for 'em," I said cheerfully. "Now get that alcohol lamp going, and after supper we'll take five hours of solid sleep. We need it."

That evening, while Molly slept under the car, I studied

Kasim's map, but without much result. It was pretty plain that we were lost, and in a bad place. Northern Arabia is a high table-land, but south of Nejd all the desert is low, spotted with salt marshes, and without any oases to speak of. Having found a bone pipe and tobacco in Kasim's clothes, I smoked a pipe, thanked God for being free again, and went to sleep.

At midnight we took up our journey, to the north this time. The motor ran smoothly, we had four days' supply of water left, and I had hopes of finding the Tamarisk Mountains, or else the Flower Country, as marked on Solomon's map. The moon was brilliant that night, being at the full.

"We are in a historical country, though unexplored," said Molly, after we had made some approach toward the northern hills. "It was down here that the legions of Ælius Gallus were sent by Augustus—and most of them stayed here."

"All right," I laughed. "If the petrol doesn't give out, maybe we'll find 'em."

I was to remember that miserable joke later.

It was easy to see why no caravan had ever crossed that awful place. Tittle whirls of wind came swooping down on the sun-dried salt dust, and scooped out hollows five or six feet deep at a time; the glittering dust would rise in the moonlight like snowflakes, and pirouette away over the plain in a diamond-glinting column, to fall away gradually to nothing. There were dozens of them, and when one of them struck us it left the car white with dust.

The ancient salt lake must have dried out thousands of years before, and the boggy places were doubtless fed by underground streams, for there was not the faintest hint of any moisture in the air.

About three o'clock we came to the hills. These were nothing but a dozen gigantic masses of bare rock, very high and wind-rounded, which stuck up from the plain. They bore no sign of vegetation or water, and our car had no trouble in winding along between them, the desert floor remaining fairly level. I had lighted the lamps in order to avoid any possibility of danger from the shadow-filled hollows, when, as we turned the corner of a rock mass, a sharp cry of alarm broke from the girl beside me.

"Look out—there's a man!"

I shut off the engine, reaching for a rifle in the same movement; in the light of our lamps the figure of a man stood out plainly against the rock, only twenty feet away. But instead of picking up the rifle, I straightened back with a gasp of amazement.

"By thunder—either that fellow has escaped from a circus, or—or—"

Without stopping to finish, I leaped out, and Molly followed me. She had noticed the same thing. For the man was leaning on a spear, and he was clad in armour; short-crested helmet, breast-plate, shield—everything was exactly as a Roman soldier in a circus is arrayed. I walked up to the figure, and then stopped suddenly, a dozen feet away, with cold sweat breaking out all over me.

The man had been dead ever since the army of Ælius Gallus had been destroyed.

There was not a shadow of doubt about it. Molly Quaintance realized what the thing was, and with a cry that sounded like a sob she turned and ran for the car. I took one look at the leathery face and hands, preserved through the centuries by the dry salt air, and, perhaps, uncovered by the wind that same night, and followed her. Without a word I climbed into the car and started off, and neither of us ever referred to that Roman soldier for a good many weeks afterward. It makes me shiver to-day, as I think of him standing there in the moonlight, a mute warning to those who came past on the road to the pit of hell. Would that we had taken the warning then and there!

But we did not, and with the morning we found the salted lands behind us and a new country ahead. It was no more hospitable, being straight desert intermixed with masses of calcined rock, granite, and basalt, but to be out of that horrible salt was a relief.

The shock of seeing that perfectly preserved two-thousand-year-old Roman must have unsettled Molly, for after our noon rest she was not at all well, and finally owned up to having a touch of fever. It seemed ridiculous in that saline, dry climate; yet it only showed how thoroughly Parrish knew his business. I was at a loss how to account for it at the time, but I gave her some quinine and pulled her up, then took a dose myself.

That afternoon we came upon another terrible thing, and one which gave us a clue to the fever mystery. At four o'clock we sighted a white patch ahead on the plain, and at first took it for a blotch of salt again. But when we drew nearer we found that it was not salt at all, but bones—thousands, millions of bones. And all were human bones.

"What's that over there?" and Molly pointed to the right, speaking in an awed voice. "It looks like a pillar, Walter!"

And it was a pillar, sure enough, badly eroded, but with Greek characters cut deeply into its eastern face. My Greek was all but gone, but Molly had gone direct from college into associated charities work, and between us we made out the important part of the inscription, and the date. Here it is, as I jotted it down at the time.

> —sect of barbarians, heretics from their own—the body of Antichrist. All save the artisans we slew—we shall preserve as a testimony before God—Bishop of Theopolis, year of God 852.

These disjointed fragments were all we could make out, but when we had finished, Molly and I stared at each other in blank amazement, hardly daring to believe our senses.

"See here," I said slowly; "you remember that conversation between your uncle and Parrish? How some of the Shiah sect of Moslems had stolen Muhammad's body. I mean? Well, you know the Shiah and Sunni, the heretics and orthodox of Islam, hate each other like poison—"

"It was true, then!" she exclaimed quickly, her eyes wide.

"Hold on!" I cried, suddenly remembering everything. "Listen here, Molly! There's a city called Theopolis—the City of God—somewhere off in the desert; it was built by the last remnant of Christian Arabs; those people met these Shiahs, who were carrying Muhammad's body back to Persia, and wiped them out. That's all a guess, but it hangs together, by thunder! And these Theopolis people preserved the body of Muhammad, whom the old Christians all called Antichrist, as 'a testimony before God'—we've hit it, Molly! By thunder, we've hit it!"

I stared into her eyes; suddenly she shivered a little, looking around.

"Doesn't if feel—damp?" she queried.

The question startled me, and brought me out of my frantic eagerness. Yes, it was undoubtedly damp—yet the desert stretched off into the horizon! I looked at the heaps of bones, realised suddenly that weapons, clothing, flesh had all vanished; then I felt a little breeze blowing from the east, across the desert.

And the breeze was damp.

Not being a scientist, I cannot give an adequate explanation of this phenomenon, which I imagine would involve the peculiar geology of the region. At the cause, however, I managed to make a shrewd guess, which was proven right later.

"Those Arab tales aren't so far off the track, Molly, and Solomon's map must have been strictly accurate. We're near the Flower Country, the Belad es Zohur; according to Solomon, that borders the quicksands, or El Akhaf. There's your swamp country, and that's where this wind is coming from. That means we want more quinine, and not nitre."

We travelled on until after sunset, covering some forty miles. When we halted on a little hillock, it was too dark to see anything far ahead, and the wind had fallen; but after becoming used to the dry hot desert, we noticed clearly that the air was moist and miasmatic and unhealthy, while shrubs and ghada bushes had increased in number and size.

Both of us were worn to the bone, so that night we turned in and slept until daybreak for the first time since our escape. When we rose in the morning, we knew at last what the Belad es Zohur meant, and why it attracted no Arab caravans.

From the hillock beside which stood our car, we had a view across some fifteen miles of desert in all directions. I say fifteen miles, because that was the approximate distance at which lay the white cross. Behind us was the desert we had crossed; to the east, running from north to south, was the Flower Country.

This consisted, first of a strip of sand varying from two to five miles in width, sometimes even more; the sand was distinctly a quicksand, having a peculiar wet sheen, while with the binoculars we could see that the sand masses quivered and shook in places like jelly. Beyond the sand, however, set like an inner ring, were the flowers. These flowers, as nearly as I could tell when I examined them later, belonged to a species of cane, and were more like parasitic excrescences on the tops of the canes than like real flowers. They were a dull red in colour, and seemed absolutely to carpet the land for miles, so thick were they. The canes or stalks were about thirty feet in height.

The whole business was exactly like a Tennessee canebrake, topped with dull-scarlet flowers and stretching for miles. The width of the flowers was from five to ten miles, and the canes themselves were yellow-brown; they grew in a nearly stagnant marsh, which provided water for the quicksands.

Now, seemingly placed on the south-eastern horizon, just showing above the red sea of flowers, and yet sharply outlined against the blue sky, was a white cross. Nothing else. No hill or building or other vestige of humanity, save that white cross rising over the flower sea. I recalled Solomon's map and that of Kasim, and the cross upon each.

"I believe we're at the end of the chase," I exclaimed excitedly, pointing it out on the map. Molly, her cheeks flushed with eagerness, nodded and raised the binoculars for another look at that weird cross.

"It looks like stone," she remarked. "Look at it, Walter."

I did so, and as nearly as I could tell, the cross was, indeed, stone. Its size must have been immense, however.

"Well, Molly, we're at the rainbow's end, I really believe. The next question is how to find Solomon and how to get across the quicksand and marsh. Kasim never had a chance to tell me, but he must have expected to meet Solomon somewhere on the edge of this quicksand."

"And do you think that is the place mentioned on the pillar?" she said slowly.

"Yes—Theopolis, the City of God. There may be people living there; there may be only ruins and skulls, but there we'll find Muhammad's body—or else there's been an awful lot of money and human life wasted for nothing!"

To tell the truth, I was just a little ashamed of the emotion which the sight of that cross aroused in me. I did not care a hang about Muhammad's body. But after those leagues of desert, after the sights we had seen, after weeks in a land where to be termed a Nazarene was a deadly insult, that beautiful great cross of white against the sky stood out like a miracle. It was uncanny, superhuman, seeming to rise out of that crimson-flower sea as it did. And as we gazed at it from that hillock, little did either of us guess the story of that cross—the story which would shake the whole world of Islam to its foundations.

"Time for breakfast," said Molly gravely, turning to me. For a moment I looked deep into her eyes, and knew that she felt exactly as I did myself.

"Yes," I nodded. "It's time for breakfast."

With which inane speech we returned to the car and said no more until we had eaten and shaken off the feeling of uncanniness and awe that rested upon us. Then, when I had my bone pipe lighted, I proceeded to take the cover from the car and stretch it over a space on the sand.

"There's no use going on," I explained. "We can't cross that quicksand and marsh, and if we go either to north or south we may miss Solomon."

"But why stay here?" asked Molly, wondering. "It's better to keep moving—"

"No." I smiled a little. "I have learned something, Molly—to put my faith in John Solomon. Kasim wasn't heading this way for nothing. That hillock above us is just the place to send up a smoke signal, and there are plenty of ghada bushes to make fire with. We have enough water for three days, if we're careful, and by digging near that quicksand I think we can get more."

After discussing the situation thoroughly, she agreed that I was right though she had little faith that Solomon would turn up to answer my smoke signal.

By noon I had made a very decent camp, gathered a few of the tree-like ghada shrubs, and, taking them to the top of the hillock, I soon had them blazing and smoking finely. There was danger that the smoke would bring Parrish on us, but that had to be risked.

The day passed slowly. With the next dawn I began to send up my signal once again, and as there was no breeze, it rose clear and straight into the sky. That second day dragged, and by sunset I was distinctly worried, though I gave Molly no sign of it.

Our stock of water had almost run out. We might possibly dig and find some, but I had nothing with which to dig except my long, crooked dagger. When the third dawn broke a new and at first ludicrous danger descended upon us.

This came in the form of a breeze from across the flower-marsh. It was cool and grateful enough as the morning sun grew blazing hot, but it was heavy with a scent of flowers—a scent which was anything but healthy. I kept myself and Molly full of quinine until our ears rang, but more or less I saw a subtle menace in the odorous heavy scent, should the breeze continue from the same quarter.

By the afternoon I was forced to admit that we were up against it. The water was nearly gone, carefully though we husbanded it, and our provisions were running low. I called Molly into frank consultation and laid the situation before her.

"That white cross seems to lie south of us," she said slowly. "Why not make a dash to the south in the car, Walter?"

"We'll have to do it," I assented gloomily. "However, let's wait till morning. If no sign of Solomon appears by then, we'll make a desperate effort to reach somewhere, and if that fails we can dig for water as a last resort. But I'm sorry. Molly, that I've got you into this mess—"

"Perhaps God sent us that cross as a sign, Walter," she said softly, and after that I said no more.

I sent up my last smoke signal at sunset hopelessly, and when Molly had retired into her shelter for the night, I sat long under the stars, smoking and facing the ugly prospect which lay ahead. When at length I rolled up, it was with little hope in my heart.

My sleep was unusually sound that night, perhaps induced by the heavy scent of that flower-marsh. The same thing brought me many dreams, until at the end I felt myself being suffocated by the iron hands of Lionel Parrish, and so woke up, coughing and catching at my throat. There was, indeed, an odd smell in my nostrils—the smell of vile plug tobacco, vaguely reminiscent. Even as I sat up and gazed at the paling stars, a quiet, chuckling voice broke in upon my wonder.

"Mornin', Doctor Firth. It's werry 'appy I am to see you, sir."

And there, sitting a yard away and smoking his old clay pipe, was John Solomon!

CHAPTER VIII

THEOPOLIS

"**D**RIED DATES is all werry well, says I, but not as a steady diet, sir and miss. Wariety is the spice o' life, as the old gentleman said when 'e kissed the new 'ousemaid."

Solomon, Molly, and I were sitting at breakfast, and I saw that Molly had taken an instant liking to the pudgy, blue-eyed little man. For that matter, I found myself overjoyed at seeing him; there was a fascination about him which was hard to resist.

He had seen our smoke the day before, and had come north on a racing camel to investigate; he had come quite alone, and we found that in playing his own hand he had been forced to use the utmost skill. The Emir of Nejd had met him and given him all he asked, but Solomon had of necessity been forced to keep the story of his quest a secret. Consequently his party of twenty picked Nejd warriors was encamped to the south; as they were, of course, Moslems, Solomon dared not hint to them the thing which he sought.

He had travelled fast and hard. Though recovered from his wound, he was worn and quite thin, but cheerful in the extreme. On tumbling into that secret passageway when surprised by Parrish at Port Said, he had promptly fled; before we reached Suez he had gotten into Arabia, had met the emir and made his dispositions, and without delay started for the Abode of Emptiness.

Nothing had been heard or seen of Parrish, but upon my telling him of the death of Graves and the intercepted note Solomon wagged his head and sucked his pipe.

"This 'ere game ain't finished," he observed at length, his wide blue eyes resting uneasily on Molly, "I'm mortal sorry, miss, as 'ow you come along, but there ain't no 'elp for it now. You'll 'ave to come with us, that's all."

"Then the story was really true?" she asked eagerly. "And the body of Muhammad—"

"Yes, miss, 'is body is over yonder," and John waved his pipe toward the white cross. We had told him about finding the pillar, and he corroborated my translation of the inscription and my guess at the meaning of it all. "This 'ere was the place where the Christian Arabs come to, sir and miss— They met up wi' them there Shiahs an' took the body o' Muhammad. They killed all the Persians except some artisans, which same they took for slaves. Them there slaves, sir and miss, 'ad no way of escape; but bein' good Moslems, they 'ad 'opes as 'ow some day the Arabs might discover where the body o' Muhammad 'ad been took to. So they made a rosary—a Molsem rosary of a 'undred beads, each bead standin' for one o' the beautiful names of Allah, as they say."

Then for the first time I recollected the beads I had taken from Parrish, and hastily stuck my hand into my pocket. Solomon continued calmly, and I waited.

"On them there beads, sir and miss, they put marks." John reached into his own pocket and brought forth his beads, still strung on their red twine. He picked out one and held it up to us. "On this 'ere side, you see, was writin' in gold wire under the lacquer; on the other side was a smaller mark showin' which o' the names of Allah the bead stood for. When all the beads is put together by colours an' sorted out, the writin' runs together, so to speak, an' tells whereabouts the body o' the Prophet lays. The Senussiyeh got on to the story, an' when Mr. Graves and I was a-tryin' to get 'old o' the beads, they went an' got some of 'em first. Dang me, that Parrish 'e's got thirty and—"

"No, he hasn't," I broke in, smiling. "He hasn't any of them, John."

"Eh?" Solomon looked at me, and his eyes suddenly widened.

"How many beads have you?" I asked, trying to keep down my excitement.

"Sixty-four," returned John.

"Then here are the rest for you," and I jerked them out and put them in his hand.

He was absolutely dumbfounded. His mouth opened and shut again, and he stared from the beads to us and back, utterly astounded. Then he flung back the hood of his burnoose, his grey hair almost white in the morning sunlight, and looked out over the marsh at the white cross, miles away.

"Thank God!" he said, slowly and reverently. That was all, but the heartfelt way in which he said it was deeply impressive.

"But what's behind it all?" I broke out suddenly. "Why the devil don't you let Parrish take the body back to Mecca, where it belongs, John? Why should we—"

His slow eyes rested on mine and struck me silent. There was a strange and solemn power in his face, as though his inner thoughts had uplifted and ennobled him; and so they had, as I verily believe.

"Doctor Firth," he said very slowly, "if so be as the Senussiyeh gets that 'ere body, 'ere's what'll 'appen. They'll take over the 'oly cities of Islam and drive the Turks out of Arabia; they'll proclaim a 'Oly War, there'll be a flame of revolt from Egypt to Morocco, from India to central Africa. Let word go out as 'ow the Senussiyeh 'olds the body o' the Prophet, and all Islam will rise, sir and miss. Just like that.

"This is the last chance o' the Senussiyeh, Doctor Firth. Once before they tried it, an' I blocked 'em. They've been a-fightin' the Italians, an' now it's do or die, so to speak. It ain't the British that's in danger, sir and miss; it's the 'ole o' Christendom, it is that! You don't know what them devils is up to, but I do; me spies 'as been watchin' of 'em; I've had me own men among 'em like poor Kasim, and if they ever get 'old o' the Prophet's body, they'll sweep the Christians out o' the 'ole Eastern world! And they'll do it, too, mind that!"

Before the little man's fierce earnestness I was silent, and cursed my own blindness in not seeing previously what was going on. Solomon was quite right. I knew how the British veneer in Egypt and India, the French rule in western Africa, the Italian grip on Libya and Somaliland—how all this was underlain by the awful volcano of Moslem fanaticism.

It would take a tremendously big thing to make this fanaticism burst forth into destruction, but the Senussiyeh was playing for that very thing. With the body of Muhammad in their hands, the tale of the empty tomb at Medina would convulse the whole Moslem world; Shiah and Sunni would unite against the infidel; the trained engineers and leaders of the order would lead Moslem armies, and there would be a terrible religious war to the death.

It was for this that the Senussiyeh had been for years collecting supplies and munitions in their monasteries and cities, sending their young men to gather the best of European and American knowledge, training them in half the armies of Europe. Did Parrish succeed, the Senussiyeh would have an appeal which would cause the British and French native armies to rise *en masse*.

And over against this was set a pudgy little Cockney with wide blue eyes.

"Good Lord!" I breathed hoarsely, staring at him. "John—what shall we do?"

"Go an' find that 'ere body," he said in a matter-of-fact way. "I 'ave some dynamite. It ain't a nice job, sir and miss, but we've got to blow Muhammad up, so to speak. We couldn't werry well carry of 'im off. I 'ave a Kodak; we'll take pictures of 'im, and there you are."

I glanced at the girl beside me. Her dark cheeks were flushed, her eyes were brilliant with excitement.

"And you know where he is buried, then?" she asked breathlessly.

"When we get these 'ere beads put together, miss, I will," said Solomon quietly. "We'd best leave this car right 'ere in case o' need. There's a way across that quicksand as I know of, so if we get to that 'ere Theopolis, destroy the body, an' get out 'o here, we'll let Parrish come an' find what 'e can."

He went on to tell us of Professor Grave's great dream. With Solomon, Graves had visited this place ten years before, ignorant of what it held. Then, little by little, the two had pieced together the story of Muhammad's body, helped by tradition and the same pillar Molly and I had found, and also by what beads they had gathered. The story of how those beads had been traced down and collected, over half the Moslem world, would have been of tremendous interest in itself, but I never learned it. Both Solomon and Graves had been working on it for years back, it seemed; without the beads, it would be hopeless to search for the body's hiding-place.

Solomon had no idea that Graves had given Parrish the real translation of the sixty-four beads that day of his death. More likely he had written the first words that came to mind in the effort to stave off the renegade, for Graves was fully aware of the importance of the thing. He had not known, however, that the Senussiyeh was also on the track, and it was this, I think, which really killed him. The shock of finding his secret known to the terrible and relentless order must have been awful.

Since the Nejd men would await Solomon's return for a week or a month or a year, he determined to lead Molly and me directly over the marsh to the city, find the body that same day, if possible, photograph it, destroy it, and then rejoin the Nejd men and leave the way clear to Parrish, if the renegade had won through. There were several roads built over the marsh and quicksand, according to Solomon, the nearest being some three miles from our present position.

So upon that we started, loading what remained of our provisions on the camel, with rifles and ammunition. Solomon had two sticks of dynamite in his bags, also, but before we started he squatted down in the sand and got out his little red notebook.

"If you'd be so good as to give me the date of Kasim's death, sir," he said, "and also that o' Professor Graves, I'll 'ave me accounts all shipshape."

I did so, and he wrote down very carefully his "accounts." Then he stuck the book away, rose, got his camel goad, roused the ugly beast to its feet, and we were off. Oddly enough, the racing camel bore a cross branded on its flank—the private mark of the emir, Ibn Rashid. Solomon had been given the finest camels from the emir's stud, which accounted for the speed he had made.

With the camel at lead behind us, we walked along the border of the quicksand, being very careful to keep clear of the quaking slithery sands themselves. As we went, Solomon told us about the city of Theopolis itself, where the white cross stood in solitary grandeur. The place was long mined, but had been of immense proportions; it was built on an island in the midst of the marsh, and curiously the builders had set their whole city underground.

"It's easy to see why they died out," I remarked, sniffing at the breeze from the east. "Any one living in the middle of that place would have a hard job keeping alive."

Yet it had been their only refuge from the hosts of Islam. And as we went along, the romance of the affair appealed more and more to my imagination. Those Persian artisans who had stolen the body of their Prophet, in the blind sectarianism of Islam, and who had afterwards been enslaved by these last remnants of Christian Arabia—those men had been true to their faith even in slavery. They had seen where their captors placed the sacred remains of Muhammad, and they had tried in their only way to give that knowledge back to the world.

I thought of how those beads had been made, by stealth and yet with cunning artificers, so that they outlasted the centuries. And who had borne them out from this deadly place? How had they finally reached the "outside"? How had they been scattered and preserved through a thousand years? When I asked Solomon about it, he gave vague answers.

"The ways o' God are werry mysterious, Doctor Firth. Them 'ere beads was scattered, but was regarded as great talismans. Some of 'em we found in Muscat, some in Persia, some in Morocco. To me own mind, the wonder of it is that we found any at all."

It was noon when we reached the causeway across the marsh, and then I began to see what a place we had come to. The causeway was formed of hewn stone, much of it broken and crumbled, and was built at a point where the quicksand was quite narrow. Solomon declared that the moist shifting sands could not be very deep, pointing out how the solid foundations of the causeway were sunk straight down and cemented firmly; even so, the labour involved must have been enormous. Out of several such roads, Solomon stated that this one was the best preserved.

Soon we were across the quicksands, and now the tail canebrake rose on either hand, crowned by its sea of flowers. The canes were quite dry, and were so thick that they formed a solid mass; here and there some had broken through the rained stones of the causeway, forcing themselves up through crevices. As a place of refuge, this city of Theopolis must have been excellent, but it must have been horribly unhealthy. Perhaps this was why the inhabitants had built their dwellings underground.

Solomon told us that twenty miles to the north were the Tamarisk Mountains, and from what I gathered then and later, it is my belief that the people of Theopolis lived mainly in those mountains, since Solomon said that they showed evidence of having been very fertile. This island itself was no doubt used as a fortification, a place of general refuge, which would be a logical explanation of its location and curious buildings.

Midway across the bridge we came to a sunken tablet, perfectly preserved, its Greek inscription as clear-cut as on the day it was chiselled. It commemorated the completion of the causeway in the year 763 by a Bishop Sergois, and small wonder. That causeway was all of twelve miles long.

The marsh and quicksands were fed from springs on the island, as we discovered, and the island itself, with the underlying strata, was solid rock. The afternoon was half gone when at length we sighted the island, but we gained no clear view of anything except the gigantic cross until we won through the last of the inclosing mass of canes and set foot upon the pavement beyond.

The place was significant in its utter bareness. Imagine a flat platform, almost exactly square and each side measuring a mile; the entire level floor covered with unbroken paving, the sides enclosed by a massive wall ten feet thick and twelve high, and in the exact centre the great cross. That was Theopolis, at first glance.

But as we advanced toward the cross we began to observe the remarkable features of the place. The stone pavement itself was bare and solid, filled with cement; but the enclosing wall was a blaze of magnificent colour. It must have been built much later than the causeway, and some idea of the work spent upon it can be gained from the fact that it completely bounded the mile-square platform.

The entire wall was faced with tiling—the same antique tiling which may be seen to-day carefully preserved in Cairo and a few places in western Africa. Beyond a doubt it was due to those same Persians who had stolen Muhammad's body and been enslaved—they were named as "artisans" upon the pillar, I remembered. This would uphold the contention of some authorities that the lost art of making these wonderful lacquered tiles originated in Persia.

However that may be, the twelve-foot wall was faced from top to bottom with an intricate maze of tiling, dazzling in its brilliant colours, and telling a continuous story in pictures and Greek text. I never had a chance to decipher it, but from what little I gathered I imagine that it was the story of Theopolis itself:

interspersed with battle scenes and portraits were many sections portraying the building of the same platform on which we stood and also the gigantic cross.

In the surface of the great pavement there were five very large openings, four set well in from each corner toward the centre, and one in the centre near the cross itself. These openings contained stone stairways, which gave on to the passages and city below, as we later found to our bitter sorrow. For the present, however, we made no attempt to explore or enter them. Solomon found a huge stone ring set into the pavement near an opening in the wall giving on another causeway, and he tethered the camel there while he walked on to the huge cross in the centre.

How that cross was constructed was something of a mystery. There had originally been a crucifix, but the image had vanished; also, the cross had formerly been plated with solid crimson tiles, of which only a few remained around the base. Instead of being stone, as I had thought, it was of cement, in which the tiles had been laid, and was probably re-enforced, since the arms were unbroken. The cross was, I imagine, over a hundred feet in height; we measured the base that evening and found it to be eight feet square, tapering gradually toward the top.

"It must have been a glorious thing, Walter, when all those red tiles were in place!" and Molly gazed up at it in admiration. "What're these things for?"

As she spoke, she touched one of a row of badly corroded green copper balls which stretched at six-inch intervals around the cross at five feet from the pavement. I examined them, but they gave no clue.

"Probably ornaments, or bosses for a rotted wooden base," I concluded, then looked up. "Turn this way—quick!"

She obeyed, then broke into a rippling laugh as she caught Solomon sighting his tiny camera at us. When he had snapped the shutter, he joined us.

"A werry mysterious place, sir and miss!" He mopped his brow, then looked up at the sky with a start of surprise. " 'Ello!

We'd best be a-making camp, Doctor Firth. Dang it, we've been an' spent longer than I thought for!"

To my astonishment, I saw that the sunset was not far away, and realized that our examination of the place must have taken a considerable time. Looking over the great stone pavement with the waving reeds on all sides, a feeling of awe crept upon me, and with good reason. We were standing where Christians had stood and worshipped a thousand years before—a lost race, whose very names had perished; yet somewhere under our feet lie the body of the Prophet Muhammad, and the clue to its hiding place lay in the pocket of Solomon.

By good fortune, I had loaded our machine-top on the camel, and now we got the light canvas up for Molly's use. None of us wanted to go down into the underground city just then, and I myself infinitely preferred sleeping in the open air. Solomon led us to the eastern boundary wall, where we found a spring of clear water gathered in a bowl set into the pavement, the water running off in a trough beneath the wall into the marsh.

And there we made our camp, with that awesome gigantic cross stretching up into the darkening sky above us and the camel grunting and rumbling to one side. The long walk tired us all, and Solomon was so absolutely exhausted that when supper was over he flung himself down on his burnoose and slept, forgetful of the beads and everything else. It was as though we were in a world out of the world, and none of us had the least thought of danger.

CHAPTER IX

PARRISH PLAYS TRUMP

FOR ONCE, John Solomon had neglected his business, and we were destined to pay dearly for it—he, most of all. We must have spent an hour or so in admiring, that afternoon, when we might have been at work and off by dark. However, no use speculating. The main point is that we did nothing except camp out overnight.

The grey sky was just becoming rosy with dawn when I was awakened by a great and furious mumbling close at hand. As I sat up, I recognized Solomon's voice. He was sitting cross-legged beside me, and on the stones in front of him were ranged the "beads of Mahomet." He was busily sorting them out, muttering away in Arabic as he did so.

"What on earth are you grunting about?" I asked.

"Morning, Doctor Firth!" He looked at me, nodding. "Why, sir, I was just repeating them 'ere ninety-nine beautiful names o' God, as the Koran tells of. And 'ere's a werry odd thing, sir! You see, these 'ere beads is diwided into three main colourings, so to speak, shading off into primary colours."

He was somewhat excited, but I caught his meaning. As he had arranged the beads before him, they were indeed in three groups of colour which shaded into each other.

"Well, mebbe you know as 'ow them 'ere names of Allah are diwided into three groups on all Moslem rosaries? One the names o' wisdom, second the names o' power, an' third the names o' goodness. That's only a small thing, but werry interesting, sir."

It was indeed interesting. Those poor Shiah slave artisans must have spent years in working out every detail of this bead rosary, which was complete even in its symbolism! Solomon was working over the beads, carefully sorting them out, and he went on, with a look of intense eagerness:

"If so be as you'll wake the lady, Doctor Firth, an' get a bit o' breakfast, I'll go on wi' this 'ere job."

I nodded, and went to the shelter. Molly had been wakened by our voices, however, and now she appeared, rosy-cheeked and with her black hair massed down over her neck. I left the water pool to her, and watched Solomon until she had finished her ablutions, and by the time I had washed up, the sun was over the horizon and she was getting breakfast.

When at length the meal was ready, we called John, and he dropped work with a sigh. We polished off the last of our food, since we expected to rejoin his Nejd men before noon, and there was no need for frugality.

As we ate, I several times thought that I detected a faint sound from somewhere beneath us. Molly and Solomon could hear nothing, however. We were seated near the central stairway in front of the cross, and rising, I approached it.

"Look out for snakes!" called the girl merrily.

"It was tiles 'e 'eard, miss," said Solomon, with a chuckle. "Probably the walking up 'ere as loosened 'em, on the ceilings below."

That struck me as a very plausible guess, the more so when I looked down the wide stone stairway. It was lined on either hand with the same pictured tiles which lined the outer wall of the great platform. In one place they were broken, and, going down a few steps, I approached the spot and pried loose one of the tiles at the edge of the break. It was a fine piece of work, looking extremely like cloisonne, and bore part of the head of a monk in white upon a dark-red background. The tile was seven inches by three in size, and extremely heavy; I put it into the inner pocket of my wool cloak, as a souvenir.

There were fifteen stone steps, the stairway being nearly fifty feet wide. Below was a stone platform extending into the darkness, and I could see only that the ceiling and sides were lined with tiles, as John had stated. Taking out my electric flash lamp, I sent a ray into the passage before me. All was darkness, emptiness, with long festoons of cobwebs hanging from the room. I speedily lost all desire to explore the place, and turned to find Molly looking down over my shoulder.

"Ugh!" She gave a shudder, taking the hand I put up to her. "What a horrible-looking place, Walter! Do you really think men ever lived there?"

"I've no doubt they died there," I returned grimly, ascending to the platform with her. "Anyhow, we'll not bother 'em. I'll be glad to finish our business and get away from here. This Theopolis is a blamed oppressive place, and bad for the nerves."

It was oppressive, for a fact, yet in its way it was wonderfully beautiful. That immense platform of hewn stone, with its great cross towering into the sky, the dry canes hedging it in on every hand, topped by the flaming sea of flowers, and the intense blue dome of the sky above—it was beautiful in a desolate, awful fashion hard to describe.

The camel was on his feet at the edge of the causeway, where we had tied him nibbling away at the flowers and cane-tops, as if he enjoyed them immensely. Molly and I rejoined Solomon, who was once more squatting over his beads.

"Looks werry good, indeed, sir and miss!" cried John eagerly. "Now, Doctor Firth, you might take pencil and paper, and copy down this 'ere writing. It'd 'elp a mortal lot, as the old gentleman said when 'e asked the 'ousemaid to be 'is third."

Laughing, I took the pencil from him, together with the red notebook, found a blank sheet, and fell to work. With the bright morning air, the sunlight, the merry eyes of Molly Quaintance, it was very hard for me to be impressed by the body of Muhammad or anything else. Even John's terrific intensity and streaming face, even the fact that his marvellous brain must be working under tremendous tension, failed to sober me very much. The whole situation seemed unreal.

Indeed, that island in the marsh gave one a sense of being apart from the world, of being cut off from mankind. At the time, I thought it nothing more than the tall canebrake which cut off all sight of the desert around, together with the effect of the great, bare pavement and the majestic cross. Yet now I know differently. I know that the feeling was some subtle emanation from below. I know that it was an indefinite sensewave which struck and set vibrating those half-guessed chords of what we call the sixth sense. No man could long remain near that hell-pit and not feel it. Well, to go on with my story:

Solomon, squatted over his beads, slowly read off to me the marks on each bead. As I have said before, these were unvowelled, and my knowledge of Arabic was too scanty to permit of my translating. Still, I could make out words here and there, so that long before Solomon had come to the end of his beads I was growing more than a little excited. Molly leaned on my shoulder, looking over at the notebook.

"What is it?" she breathed eagerly.

Solomon caught the low words, and looked up. His blue eyes were very wide, and his lips trembled a little.

"Miss, just you wait!" he said huskily. "This 'ere is a-going to bust the 'ole Moslem world wide open when it gets out—just like that, sir an' miss!"

He would say no more, but leaned forward again. The beads were strung out in a long line across the stones, and by matching the graduated colours he was enabled to get them in proper order; more especially as, while he worked, he kept mumbling to himself the "beautiful names of Allah." I He seemed to know them as accurately as any sheikh in Islam. I wrote down the symbols as he read them off to me, and finally he took the last bead, the largest of all, and cried out hoarsely:

"Allah! And nothin' on the other side—give me that 'ere notebook, sir!"

Squatting beside him, I handed him the book in feverish excitement. He seized it, and leaned forward, then uttered another sharp cry.

"Dang it—I've been an' made mistakes! 'Ere, Doctor Firth, you take it down again, and be werry careful!"

So, carefully examining the tiny marks corresponding with the names of Allah, he once more went over the hundred beads, one by one; and once more I wrote down the Arabic characters. Then, finishing, Solomon scrambled to his feet, mopped his streaming face, and seized the notebook.

He demanded the pencil, and fell to work hastily, jotting in vowels where they should be, changing a line here and another there until he had transformed the script into present-day Arabic. His knowledge of the tongue must have been nothing short of marvellous, for he worked rapidly and at high tension.

"That's right, that's right!" he exclaimed, and shoved the notebook into my hand. "Where's that 'ere camera?"

Finding this, he turned and walked away in haste, until he was halfway to the boundary wall. Then he turned and took a picture, apparently of the towering cross. We watched him in wondering silence until he returned to us, panting.

"You see, sir and miss," he explained hurriedly, "we've got to 'ave records of this 'ere thing. Dang it, I'm a-going to smash the 'ole danged Moslem faith! I'm a-going to make that there Prophet a laughing-stock all over the East! Why, it's real poetic justice, it is that; 'e'sbeena-laying 'ere under this 'ere cross for a thousand year, and the Moslems will go fair wild! Dang it, I'm a-going to bust 'em wide open!"

"But what does the blamed thing say?" I demanded hotly. "Translate it, man!"

My words calmed him, and once more he was his usual unobtrusive phlegmatic self. He pulled out his pipe and whittled it full, his fingers trembling visibly; when he had it drawing well, he carefully tore away the leaf containing my Arabic writing, then handed back the notebook and pencil.

"Now, sir, if you'll be so good as to write down what I say?"

So, with Molly watching breathlessly every movement of the pencil, I wrote in English the message which had been so weirdly fashioned by those Shiah artisan slaves a thousand years before. And here it follows, word for word as I took it down. The Arabic is not unlike shorthand, when written, and I suppose Solomon had expanded the condensed and abbreviated symbols; besides, a hundred beads can carry a good deal of a message:

> In the name of God, the Merciful!
> In the Abode of Emptiness is a city of Nazarenes, wherein stands a great cross, accursed be the name! Seek ye here for the Prophet of God, who sleeps beneath the cross in Nazarene mockery. On the cross are knobs of copper. Press the third knob from the north, on the side toward Mecca. Accursed are we who stole the holy body from Medina, we and our children!
> In the name of God, the Compassionate!

It was finished. Molly's hand stole into mine, and together we stared at John Solomon, who puffed silently at his pipe. Then we all looked at the base of that cross; as it happened, we were even then standing on the western face, the side toward Mecca. I looked at the copper knobs at the north end of this face, and saw that while the first and second were corroded into more green patches, the third and those following seemed to be fairly round and firm.

Yet for a moment none of us moved. I believe that Solomon felt the same curious awe and hesitation which crept over me at the thought of disturbing this resting place of Muhammad, one of the greatest men of all the world. And as I stared at it, I realised what a terrible mockery it had been—sheer poetic justice, as Solomon had said—that the body of the Prophet had lain under that great cross of the true God long after those who builded the place were gone and forgotten of men. Yes, when this thing was made known it would split asunder the whole great mass of Islam—a religion sensitive above all else to mockery and ridicule. I understood fully why Solomon had brought that camera. And now I knew what he had meant by my "duty as a Christian gentleman"—and why he had returned to the East. John Solomon meant to destroy Islam.

Suddenly he cleared his throat and knocked out his pipe. He was quite calm now, and took the little camera from its case.

"Now, Doctor Firth," he said almost apologetically, "if you'll be so good as to press that 'ere knob, why, I'd like werry much to 'ave a picture o' what happens."

"Nothing will happen," I said thoughtfully. "If pressing the knob opens a secret chamber, the wheels and so on will have rusted away long before this."

Molly looked blank, and so did Solomon for an instant. Then his blue eyes widened a little as he stared at me.

"Doctor Firth, do you see that 'ere cross?" he said slowly, looking up at the towering shaft of white against the blue sky. "Well, sir, I put a mortal lot o' faith in that there symbol."

The rebuke was a solemn one, and I had nothing more to say. As if somewhat ashamed of his own display of emotion, however, Solomon went on more lightly:

"Besides, sir and miss, this 'ere stone paving looks werry right an' tight, it does that."

I was silenced. For a fact, I could see no break in the stones, and knew that he must be correct. No matter where the body had been hidden, it must be well-preserved from the damp, and the secret machinery with it. Those builders were no fools, as their solid work showed clearly.

Upon approaching the face of the cross closely, I noticed that the pediment was some eight feet high, and, as I had formerly conjectured, had at one time been covered with some kind of wood. About the bottom of the pediment were heaped fallen tiles and rubble from the cross above.

Smiling a little at my own hesitation, I walked up to the third knob from the end, while Solomon stood with camera ready, an anxious look upon his face, and Molly watched in tensed waiting. Shrinking a little as I did so, I touched the boss, half expecting it to vanish suddenly. Nothing happened, however.

The copper boss was corroded solidly into its place, beyond a doubt. I pressed it with all my strength, then tried to twist and wrench it, but it seemed as solid as the cement in which it was set.

" 'It it!" cried Solomon hoarsely. " 'It it 'ard!"

I would like to write of that moment as solemn and awesome, but it was not. I was excited, and obeyed Solomon, hitting the boss hard. In consequence I skinned my fist, and promptly hit the boss again angrily. When I got through saying things, I found Molly holding out one of the tiles, and laughing openly.

"Hit it with this," she chuckled, and stepped back.

Ashamed of my own taut nerves, which had caused the outburst, I swung with the tile and smashed it against the copper boss with all my strength. The tile shattered into fragments, then I caught Molly's warning cry:

"Look out, Walter! It's moving!"

Luckily for myself, I leaped backward instantly; that last blow had done the business. There was a sound of splintering, rending cement and stone, then the whole face of the great pediment seemed to leap out at me bodily; a second later, it was sinking into the pavement, slowly and surely.

We stared at it, transfixed. Molly's hand was gripping mine, and we heard the "click-click" of the camera shutter as Solomon "snapped" it. With a crashing jar the huge pediment face sunk flush with the pavement and stopped. Where it had been was a chamber; the whole base of the pediment was hollow, and in it reposed a long sarcophagus of stone.

Probably it had never been disturbed since the day it was sealed up. On the side of the coffin were Greek letters, deeply chiselled; but beneath these, rudely scrawled in Arabic characters, were the painted words, "Muhammad ibn Abdallah. God is God, and Muhammad the Prophet of God!" The chiselled

Greek spelled only the words, "The Antichrist." It was the tomb of Muhammad.

None of us dared speak for a moment, though I heard the camera click again. For my own part, that painted inscription struck fire from my soul, as I thought of those faithful Persian slave artisans. It was they who had done the work, no doubt; by stealth and in secret they had built the mechanism, and at the last moment had added that scrawl in honour of their Prophet. And, after a thousand years, their bead rosary had borne its message to the world, but not as they had hoped. Their labour and sweat and death had only brought about the destruction of their religion, it seemed in that moment.

"Let's 'ave the lid off, Doctor Firth!"

I stepped forward, as John advanced, and with something approaching reverence we gripped the stone lid of the sarcophagus and heaved it back. A crash, a little dust, and we were staring down at the features of Muhammad ibn Abdallah. Molly joined us timidly.

The body was mummified, or else preserved in some fashion. While the face was shrunken and dark, I could still make out the noble outline of the features and high brow. Arab writers have written that Muhammad was buried with one hand under his face, looking toward Mecca, and so in truth we found him.

"By thunder!" I ejaculated softly. "These Christian Arabs carried their refined mockery out clear to the end, Molly! Not content with labelling him Antichrist and burying him under this great cross, they faced him toward Mecca—what devils they must have been!"

Strangely enough, my sympathy lay entirely with the body of this great man who had founded an alien creed. Solomon nodded at my words, as Molly turned away, unable to look further at the body.

"Now, let's 'ave that 'ere coffin up on its side, sir," said John. "I want a good picture of 'im as 'e lays, then we'll finish it and be off."

Conquering my natural revulsion, I helped John turn the stone coffin over so that the open face pointed toward the light, and we rearranged the body within. Even at that moment I found myself wishing that I could examine the remains and see what form of preservation had been used, but there was no time for that.

Solomon stepped off toward the wide stairway, while I joined Molly to one side of him, watching. Twice the shutter clicked, then John looked up.

"There!" and he sighed, trembling as he stood. "I'll smash that 'ere Moslem—"

"Thank you, Mr. Solomon!"

At the cold, cruel voice, we whirled. A lean, powerful hand had snatched the camera from John's hand, and behind the revolver touching his neck was the exultant face of Lionel Parrish. Two men were covering me with rifles, and up the stairway were clambering half a dozen more of Parrish's men.

The Senussiyeh had struck!

CHAPTER X

I BECOME VENTURESOME

"**V**ERY KIND of you, Mr. Solomon, very kind indeed! You see, we've been here for two days, now, waiting until you came and opened up the tomb for us—cracked the nut, so to speak, that we might take the kernel."

Molly had shrunk to my side, and held to my arm, fascinated. Parrish stood there like a king, satanically handsome and regal and arrogant, holding his revolver against Solomon's neck, smiling cruelly. But John made no offensive movement. White as a sheet, he looked into the brown eyes of Parrish, and held silence.

Eight men in all, one of them wounded, had gathered behind Parrish at the head of the great stairway. With a quick order, Parrish tossed the camera to them. One of them brought down his rifle butt upon the box, smashing it into splinters.

A hoarse cry broke from Solomon and the renegade's trigger finger tightened. But John stood very quiet, trembling a little, his face terrible to see.

"You were waiting here for us?" I asked quickly. Parrish glanced at me.

"Exactly, Doctor Firth. You very nearly discovered us this morning, when you came down those stairs! Lucky thing for you that you didn't. It pays to have patience, eh? Again, I must thank you for solving our problem so neatly."

I could not but feel tremendously sorry for John Solomon in that moment. At the very culmination of all his labour, the cup had been dashed from his hands. He had seen himself triumphant, had visualised how his story and photographs would strike at the very base of the growing menace of Islam—and then that same menace had arisen out of the depths and smitten him. Bitterest of all, Parrish had outwitted him again, had let him do all the work and was now claiming the fruits of victory.

Involuntarily I found myself wishing that I had indeed discovered the lurking danger that morning. True, I might have paid for it with my life, but Parrish would never have secured the body of Muhammad. Now it was too late. The renegade held everything in his grip, including us. And there was no mercy in his cold eyes and iron mouth. Solomon recognised it as well as I, and for a moment looked up at the cross towering majestically into the sky above. I saw his lips move a little. Then his gaze came back to Parrish.

"Colonel Parrish, if so be as you'd reach into my coat pocket an' take out the book what's there—"

With a swift frown, Parrish obeyed slowly. He drew out John's red notebook, and Solomon directed him to a certain page quite calmly. The renegade read carefully.

"Your accounts with me, eh?" He looked up, with a quick sneer, his eyes glittering like the eyes of a snake. "You're very thorough in your methods, my friend. However, I am going to settle this account very shortly. Your death will wipe it out, I fancy."

"No, sir," returned Solomon stolidly. Parrish glanced at him again.

"Eh? What do you mean?"

"My death ain't mentioned, Colonel Parrish. If so be as you'll glance at the top o' the page, you'll see as that 'ere account ain't in my name."

Parrish swept his eyes back to the page. I never knew what was written there, though I could make a shrewd guess. His face went absolutely livid, and, with a terrible curse, he tore the book across.

"Damn you!" he burst out. "Your God isn't my god, you fool!

If I didn't have a worse fate ready for you, I'd shoot you like the dog you are!"

"Dogs is werry faithful animals, sir," said Solomon steadily, his wide blue eyes never changing. "I was born a Christian, Colonel Parrish. If you'd been an' took a lesson from dogs, sir, you—"

Parrish struck him across the mouth, and he staggered. The renegade was in a mad fury for a moment; then, with an effort, he quieted himself, and those inhuman brown eyes settled upon Solomon's face.

For all their cold power, for all their hypnotic quality, they failed of their purpose; Solomon's mild blue eyes would not down, and he faced the renegade quietly, a little trickle of blood running from his mouth. How long that conflict of wills endured I cannot say, but in the end Parrish turned away with a curt order to two of his men:

"Bind this infidel!"

They advanced and obeyed the order. Solomon made no resistance, but his voice lifted again to Parrish, who had turned his back:

"This 'ere cross 'as lasted a mortal long time, Colonel Parrish, and it'll last a good while longer—"

The renegade spat out a word, and one of the Arabs struck Solomon again, so that he stood quiet, his arms bound behind him. I think that Parrish had been hit in a vital spot, however; for a space he remained standing looking out across the great pavement, motionless.

His eight men stood awaiting their orders, and their faces were as pitiless as that of their master. They were all of the same type, cruel and inhuman and beyond any thought of mercy. Then Parrish swung around on us, and he was once again his cold evil self, kingly in his devilish way, smiling with no mirth in his eyes.

"Well, well, Solomon! So you've got the body of the Prophet for me, eh? That is a very good turn, my man, and I'll remember it. By the way, Doctor Firth has told you about that note I intercepted?"

Solomon nodded slightly. The renegade's eyes flashed to me for an instant, and I was afraid. He had not forgotten our little scrap, by any means.

"Yes, sir,'e told me. And 'ow did you make out getting 'ere, if I may ask?"

"It took a fight, I'll admit," returned Parrish evenly. "But we got here."

Solomon looked at the eight men, and I thought a sudden light came into his expressionless eyes for a fleeting moment.

"Yes, sir," he answered quite humbly. "But I thought as 'ow you 'ad more men than these 'ere, Colonel Parrish."

"I had," and there was no mistaking the spasm of fury which contracted the face of the other man. "But they're gone, Solomon, and so are the Nejd men who attacked me. So you see I have a little debit account on my own side of the ledger. An account in blood, my friend, and it will be paid in blood."

"Yes, sir, I'm afraid it will," assented John, quite as a matter of course. "But, Colonel Parrish, I'd be werry much obliged if so be as you'd let me do all the payin', so to speak. This 'ere young lady 'adn't ought to be dragged into our—"

Molly's hand tightened on my arm, as Parrish broke in with a cold sneer. I stole a glance at her face, and it was white but brave—so brave that it heartened me.

"No use, Solomon. She and Doctor Firth have seen too much. Besides, I've a small account of my own with Doctor Firth, and I've found a very nice method of settling it. There's a little place down below where I'm going to stow you away—"

He looked up, at a sudden noise. Solomon's camel had pulled free and was calmly and in most dignified fashion walking along the causeway back toward solid land. Parrish seemed about to give an order, when John cut in hastily with a remark which drove all thought of the camel from the renegade's head:

"By the way, Colonel Parrish, if you'd 'ave your men turn over that 'ere coffin, there's summat carved on it which you could translate to them with advantage to yourself, so to speak."

Parrish at once ordered two of his men to the sarcophagus. They knew whose the body was, for as they approached it both went to their knees for a moment; then, putting their strength to the stone coffin, they turned it upright again, and Parrish saw what had been carven on the side.

I thought that he would shoot John where he stood, for his revolver came up like a flash. But he stuck it away in its holster and walked over to the chamber in the pediment of the cross where he stood for a space, gazing down on that which had been the greatest Arab who ever lived.

While he stood thus, with his back toward us, I looked again at Molly and met her brave, violet eyes. Now, because I thought that presently I would die, I made no secret of that which was in my heart.

"I'm sorry, dear," I murmured softly. "It looks pretty bad, and for your sake I'm sorry. I love you, Molly dear."

Our eyes met. The colour flooded into her dark cheeks and then out again, but in the clear steady eyes all the girl's sweet soul spoke forth bravely, even before her lips opened:

"Kiss me, Walter—before it comes. I love you, too."

And there, while those vulture-eyed brethren of the Senussiyeh looked on, I bent my face over hers, and we kissed.

Perhaps it was that kiss, perhaps it was some transfusion of spirit from brave John Solomon; but in that instant the fear left me. After all, Lionel Parrish was but a man, whom I had held in my hands and broken, and I swore inwardly that if the chance came to me I would break him again, and spare not.

That devil must have been a mind reader. He turned around and whipped out an order to the two men who had bound John. They stepped over to me and removed my weapons, though they left me unbound.

I had seen nothing of Sidi Akhbar or the other aides, and supposed that they had perished with the rest of Parrish's force. Now, however, at another order, one of the men left his rifle and went down the wide stairway, while we waited. He was gone for perhaps ten minutes, during which time we stood there in the sweltering sunlight, and none of us broke the silence.

Finally there came slow, lagging steps on the hidden stairway, and groans. Into sight came the man again, and leaning on him was Sidi Akbbar. I was shocked by the aide's appearance. He was almost lifeless, and coughed blood continuously. Without waiting for Parrish to speak, I stepped forward and helped the man lower him beside the stairway, setting him against the low parapet. His head rolled for a moment, then he gathered strength and looked up, his sunken eyes horrible.

A brief examination showed that he had been shot through the lungs, evidently some time before since the wound was inflamed and in a terrible condition. He was beyond all hope, and I said so in English. Parrish merely nodded.

"Sidi Akhbar, and you *khuan* of the Senussiyeh," he said coldly, "yonder lies the body of Muhammad ibn Abdallah, on whom be the blessing of Allah!"

Sidi Akhbar coughed out a low word, and the others joined in the first sura of the Koran—a prayer strangely similar, verse for verse, with the Lord's Prayer. When it was done, Parrish strode over beside us and pointed to Solomon.

"Set that dog on his knees before the prophet of Allah!"

A fleeting convulsion swept over John's face as two men seized him. He resisted quietly but stubbornly, until Parrish deliberately kicked him heavily in the side. With a low groan, he gave way, and was forced down on his face. Then, with a terrible coughing cry, Sidi Akhbar reeled to his feet and drew a revolver.

I thought he meant to murder Solomon, and so he did, Parrish offering no objection. But the man was too far gone, and the effort of rising had exhausted him. Twice he tried to lift his weapon, but failed, and it dropped from his nerveless hand.

"God is God, and Muhammad is the Prophet—of—" He swayed, fell on the stones, and was dead. Fanatic though he was, Sidi Akhbar was a brave man, and no renegade.

"The name of Akhbar ibn Zalib shall be inscribed on the

books of the grand lodge of the Order," said Parrish slowly, and a flash of exultation passed across the faces of the remaining eight. This, I took it, was some great honour.

The renegade's kick must have hurt Solomon sorely, while the utter brutality of it wakened all the slow anger within me. I was never a venturesome man in the old life, but I think this relapse into mediaeval barbarism must have wakened all the primitive man hate deep in my heart. As I watched Parrish, I felt my fingers curling together and tensed once more; he was looking down at Solomon now, half sneering in his triumph; and but for Molly's hand I might have gone at him then and there, careless of the rifles.

Yet that little hand on my arm gave me caution. I remembered that twenty Nejd men were waiting somewhere on the mainland, and that they would serve Solomon to the death; also, there was the camel which had departed leisurely. To be sure, ten or fifteen miles across that causeway to the mainland would be a long walk for a camel, nibbling by the way, yet if we could stave off the crisis for—

"You fool!" rang out the bell-like voice in biting scorn, and again the renegade kicked the prostrate Solomon, standing over him in arrogance and with a burst of triumph in his tone. "Get up, you fool! So you would set your hand against the Senussiyeh, eh? You beat me once, fool, but this time I win! Where is your boasted God now? Get up, you fool, who thought to cheat the Senussiyeh!"

Again he kicked the prostrate figure. Poor Molly had turned away, her hands over her face; I felt myself trembling, yet I forced myself down into quiet. It was beginning to dawn upon me that this devil would not spare even Molly, but that if one of us could get away there might yet be an atom of hope. The great stairway was only a dozen paces from me. And yet to desert Molly—

Slowly, slowly Solomon raised himself from the stones. The grey pallor of his anguished face was awful to look upon, yet behind it all was a peculiar steadiness, as though some inner faith and power had lifted him above his mental and physical suffering. He straightened up, until his tortured eyes struck full upon the face of Parrish.

"Colonel Parrish," he said slowly, "as sure as that cross is standing 'ere, the God you've blasphemed will make you answer for what you've been an' done. 'E's werry slow an' patient in 'Is ways, sir—"

He had no chance to say more, for Parrish, in a flame of fury, snatched a rifle from the nearest man and struck him over the head with the barrel. Solomon fell like a log, mercifully unconscious. Parrish whirled on me with a snarl; the devil in him was fully let loose, and again Molly caught at my arm in fear.

"If there's a scrap," I murmured softly in her ear, "you run for that stairway, and dodge the bullets." She nodded slightly.

"Doctor Firth, you have interfered in affairs too weighty for your intelligence," and the renegade's bitter voice I ashed me like a whip. His cold brown eyes were like swords, and held me transfixed with their hypnotic glitter for a space.

"You're a very strong man physically, doctor," he went on. "Mentally, it is otherwise. You are a bigger fool than Solomon, who at least is an antagonist worthy of the name."

With an effort, I swept my brain clear of his terrible influence. He had come quite close to me, and as I saw my chance approaching I grew more cautious. There was a bare hope that Molly could reach the stairway, yet her escape was a secondary matter. She could do nothing in that blackness below ground, and would be overtaken at once; criminally cowardly as it might seem, I must get away myself at all costs.

It came hard, for, like all men, I am afraid of cowardice. Still, if I did escape, I had some slight hope of rescuing her and Solomon from this devil, and to throw my life away would avail her nothing.

"Well, if I remember rightly, you found me a rather decent antagonist not long ago," I replied, with a little laugh, and the words drew a furious flame of rage from Parrish. He came still closer, until his terrible eyes were glaring into mine.

"Do you know how you're going to die, Doctor Firth? It won't be a pleasant death, I assure you. It's one that was invented long ago by men of your own faith for men of my faith, from what I can discover, and it is only poetic justice that the three of you should—"

I realized that he had chanced upon some hell hole down below and designed it for us all; the thought drove murder into my heart. My hands had been under my burnoose, and I had quietly drawn out the heavy tile, which I had picked from the staircase wall that morning. While he was still speaking, I jammed the sharp corner of it straight up into his cheek and jaw with all my strength.

His words swept into a scream, and he fell back, with the blood spurting. As he fell, I tore the revolver from his holster and leaped at the eight men behind. My only thought was to break through them, and I caught them off guard. Before their rifles were up, I shot the first man through the body and leaped over him while he was falling.

Poor Molly had been more surprised than any one, and made no motion to follow me, luckily for herself. Yet I was not to escape scot-free. Just as I gained the stairway a rifle crashed out behind and the bullet tore through my headdress, half stunned me, and sent me sprawling down the stairs.

It saved my life, for I could hear the other bullets sing and spatter over me as I went plunging down. Gaining the bottom, I had sense enough to roll over toward the dark entrance beyond, and in the moment I lay quiet before springing up, a bullet struck the stones under me and scraped along the ribs of my left side.

I sprang up, stung with pain, to see the top stairs lined with shooting men. A leap took me back into the darkness, whence I emptied my revolver up the stairway. One figure came down head-first, with a yell, his rifle clattering at my feet; I dropped my empty revolver, seized the larger weapon, and went back into the darkness at a run. As I went, however, I heard the voice of Parrish rising, and knew that I had only scotched the snake.

Then the blackness of the pit had swallowed me up.

CHAPTER XI

EX TENEBRIS VOX

T HE ONLY thought in my mind was vengeance.

Parrish would not spare Molly and John Solomon. He was an absolutely dehumanised monster, driven by that infernal Senussiyeh, and any thought of sex or pity was far from him. Yet he had said himself that we were to die by some horrible death he had discovered in the bowels of this hidden city, and this constituted my only remaining hope, though it was scant enough. It meant that there was time, and time was what I prayed for.

The renegade had been too cruel to shoot us down, unfortunately for himself. He knew that if he simply left us behind and marched away, our doom would be certain; we were in the Abode of Emptiness, and even on the mainland there was no chance that we could get away. All this, of course, leaving out the Nejd men and my own abandoned machine, things which did not enter into his calculations for reasons which I discovered later.

Having reached here two days before us, Parrish must have seen my signal fire, guessed that Solomon was at hand, and then had waited, like the inscrutable devil he was, until Solomon had unravelled the whole secret for him. In those two days the renegade had doubtless explored the underground city very thoroughly. According to his own words, he had chanced upon some torture room, where the Christian Arabs of Theopolis finished off their enemies, and intended to leave Solomon there, and Molly Quaintance.

There was no pursuit, it seemed, as I fled away into the darkness. Shaken with my fall down that stone stairway, dazed by the bullet sear across my scalp, and with fire darting through my hurt side, I went reeling and staggering on in blindness until I came slap up against a stone wall and dropped like a wounded bird.

Coming to myself, I found my head lying in a little puddle of water which came dripping from the roof above. At the moment it seemed sent by God: later, I conjectured that I lay beneath the spring and pool in the rock pavement above. It is curious how, in times of stress, men place blind faith in a guiding deity, only to seek out so-called "natural" causes when the time of stress has passed! Yet I have ever thought that through all which followed my hand was clutched by something beyond a mere guiding fate. Even in these very happenings some higher will may have been working its supreme vengeance upon Lionel Parrish.

After bathing and examining my wounds, I found that both were painful but very slight: my fall had shaken me up rather badly, however. From where I lay I could see the dim light of the entrance; it was unbroken by figures, nor did any sound come to my ears, so that I knew pursuit was checked. Had my swoon been guessed at, all would have ended very differently, but Parrish no doubt thought that I would meet a bad enough fate if left to wander about in the darkness.

Such a thing was very far from my intention, as I reflected on my position, sitting there in the puddle of dripping water. In my captured rifle's magazine were ten cartridges, and I had a pocketful of dried dates; with food, water, and ammunition, I could command the entrance from where I sat.

"Coward's thought!" I muttered angrily. "This situation demands action—not passive waiting."

I still had my match-box and the same flashlamp I had taken from Parrish. What was a great deal more important. I suddenly recalled a very obvious fact. The stairway by which my entrance had been made was the central one of five; I hastily figured that a short quarter-mile would take me to one of the comer stairways, and as each of these seemed to have its own causeway across the marsh and quicksand, I would have no difficulty in fetching the Nejd men. Excitement began to grow upon me as my course of action took shape within my brain.

It must now be past noon, so I promptly made a lunch from a few of my dates, drank my fill of the water, filled my pipe, and rose. The whole plan was coming to me now in beautiful shape! With luck, I would gain one of the other stairways before dark, slip out, and get away, reach the mainland before daybreak, and bring the Nejd men with morning—if I found them. There was no great haste, I calculated; Parrish knew nothing of the twenty Nejd men, and would be shrewd enough to make a thorough examination of the underground city, that he might return with a full report upon it.

Molly's kiss was still sweet upon my lips and sweeter in my soul. With the remembrance of the camel, new hope came to me. Perhaps the Nejd men would take warning from the beast; perhaps, on the other hand, he had gone by a different causeway, and would never be found. So thinking, I flashed on the electric lamp and pressed the stationary clasp in place, so that the light remained steady.

I had reached the end of the passage. To my right was a wide entrance, to my left another: both were lined with the pictured tiles, and as there was no difference between them, I went to the right, slinging my rifle over my shoulder by its carbine strap.

The branch passage was some twenty feet in width, and I came to a doorway at about the same distance from the entrance. Naturally, I looked in, sweeping my light in front of me. The white beam struck upon a row of grinning skulls, with other rows below and above it, whereupon f passed on without stopping. Two more doorways showed the same thing, and I realized that I had struck the cemetery portion of Theopolis.

To judge by the feet-worn stone floor, these passages and

chambers had been cut from the living rock, and later the walls and ceilings had been tiled, probably after the capture of those Persian artisans. All were very garish in colourings, yet the pictures shown were all religious or warlike. Here and there I came to memorial tablets standing out from the tiles; I did not pause for any translating, but noted some of the dates in passing. The earliest of these, if I remember rightly, was 685 A.D., so that, allowing for the time consumed in this truly gigantic work, Theopolis must have been founded by the remnants of Christian Arabs shortly after the rise of the Islamic power to the west.

Unfortunately for me, the passage was not straight, by any means. It curved and crooked about, branch passages shot off here and there, and the smoke from my pipe was borne away by a steady draught. Consequently there must be outlets, I calculated, and, after a little, I came upon one of those outlets.

After passing several doorways, I came to a curve and found a large entrance to my right. The lamp showed that the chamber was bare; but it was also lighted by a vague daylight, which I investigated. This gleam from the outer world came in at one corner, where was a long sloping passage, three feet square, pointing down. Outside this, I made out a brownish mass, together with the rippling glimmer of water, and could hear the swish of canes; the passage gave through the walls on the marsh.

It occurred to me that I might let myself slide out, but I would have no manner of climbing the walls to the great pavement, so I turned about and went back to the passage in no little disappointment. The slit in the wall was no more than a dumping way for garbage, I suppose; at all events, it offered no way of escape.

It was after this that I completely lost track of where the way led me. The main passage had grown smaller, and I suddenly noted that the tiled ceilings and walls had given way to the bare rock; whether the passage itself had thus degenerated or whether I had wandered out of it I cannot say. Since my only hope was to go forward until I reached one of the stairways. I went on.

My watch had been broken in my fall, and there was no way

of judging time left to me. At length the passage was grown so small that in desperation I struck into one of the branches. After that, I was lost indeed.

This branch passage curved and twisted, but I had long since lost all sense of direction. Of a sudden I found, to my great surprise, that it led out to one of the main arteries again—one of the large, tiled passages, such as I had struck at first. Here I paused, in doubt. Which way led to the staircase?

From what I had already discovered, these larger passages all connected with stairways; for all I could tell, this might be the very one by which I had entered. A brilliant method of settling this last question occurred to me, and I proceeded to examine some of the chambers opening on the passage. I could soon tell whether this was the cemetery again or not.

It was not, as I found upon entering the first doorway to which I came. The room was very large, and as I stepped inside I came upon a small, exhausted battery for a flashlight exactly similar to which I carried. This proved that Parrish and his men had been before me, and that he had come completely equipped for anything he might find, as he could have known nothing of an underground city. Also, it gave me some hope that the staircase was not far away, though this was soon enough dispelled.

The chamber in which I now stood had been nothing less than the workshop of those same Persian artisans—and of their children for generations, no doubt. Had I been a scientist, the secret of those tiles might have been reconstructed for the world; but I could make nothing of the heaps of clay and the utensils, most of which were only smears of rust. In one comer was a firing furnace of stone, with a flue for smoke, which seemed to lead out through the walls; on every band stood piles of tiles, finished or unfinished. I picked up one, and still have it; the thing is of solid crimson lacquer, with the Greek letters "Theos" on its face in gold, and very beautiful.

Finding nothing of interest here, in my present state of mind, I returned to the passageway and set forth again along its indeterminate windings. I investigated one more room, and found it empty of aught save a woman's skeleton in one corner, and after that all my attention was given to finding some way of escape from my predicament.

The bitter realisation began to dawn upon me that this situation might easily prove the end of me. I was lost in a blind maze of rock-hewn passages, all of which were large and crooked, and seemingly endless. My wounds were giving me a good deal of pain, and I had found no more water. Indeed, thirst began to torment me the moment the thought entered my mind.

I had failed to take warning, however, of the greatest danger of all, though plain warning had been given me by the finding of that exhausted battery. Therefore, I was in no way prepared for it when my flash-light suddenly went out. The battery was run down!

No sooner did I realize what had happened than the terrible thing absolutely unmanned me. Since early that morning I had been strung to the highest tension—first by the discovery of Muhammad's body, and later by the horrible scene with Parrish. Even through my wanderings I had been keyed up to the discovery of something unexpected at each step. With a snap, my nerves gave way.

Screaming out, I tried to run, feeling for the tiled walls with my fingers. An abrupt turn brought me smash into a wall, hurt my head cruelly, and left me crumpled up on the floor. When I came to myself I was crying like a child.

The darkness was horrible, pressing down like a real substance. For a space all hope went out of me. Still sobbing, I came to my feet and went forward blindly; after perhaps ten minutes I paused with some abruptness. For no tangible reason, I put forth a foot and felt—nothing! A faint sound of running water came to me, and with cold sweat breaking out on my brow, I drew forth a match and struck it.

Directly before me was a cavity in the floor, running sheer down. It was only some four feet square, and I edged my way around before the match gave out. Then I stood in the darkness trembling, with a horrible fear upon me. What if there were more of these murderous holes? I dared not explore farther.

The hysteria of fear gradually left me, and my shattered nerves became quiet. Counting over the matches in my pocket, I found there were but six. Fortunately I had saved the flash-lamp, and now remembered that with time for recuperation the battery would eventually give me a trifle more service. It and the matches I must keep at all costs.

"This is a hell of a fix for a decent American physician!" I said aloud.

The words went rumbling and rocking down the corridors in wild echo, and, oddly enough, the reverberations gave me heart. For a space I stood and talked to myself, saying nothing very coherent, wishing only to hear the sound of my voice in the blackness. Then I raised the rifle and fired twice.

Blind panic seized on me before the keen echoes of the shots had died away. What if Parrish, up above, heard those shots! The remembrance of what I was doing here came upon me anew; John Solomon depended on me, and so did Molly. My business was to get out of this hole, not to fall into the mad panic of a child over nothing more than being lost in the darkness.

For a moment I cursed myself for a fool, then I gathered myself together and started off—though gingerly. The savage battle with men had passed into a more savage struggle against the fear of darkness; a struggle against the most primitive of all human horrors. It struck the last remnant of civilisation out of me. Feeling my way step by step, I ate a few dates as I went, though swallowing came hard for lack of water.

Hours must have passed, but with their passing my brain and nerves grew firmer and better controlled. I must have wandered for miles, because my feet were very sore and my leg muscles weary. My only idea was a grim resolve to keep going until I dropped, and I came very near doing it. Yet all the time the elemental brute was rising in me, in a way I can scarce remem-

ber now without a shudder. That is my only excuse for what I
did a little later—that, and the bitter extremity of my position.

My exhaustion must have been great, for when I had come
upon a pool of water and lapped it up like a dog, I felt like a
man re-made. Then it occurred to me that this must be the same
puddle I had found at first, since there was but the one spring
of water on the rock surface above! In this I proved wrong, for
upon lighting one of my precious matches in wild excitement,
the water was shown to be seeping through from the side of the
passage-way instead of coming from the roof; also the passage
gave no sign of a stairway beyond.

The water gave me new life, and the incident gave me new
hope, none the less. It was, I suppose, an hour later when I came
upon the two men.

Just as I turned a bend, the flicker of light reached me from a
doorway on my right, six feet ahead. For a moment I stood still,
wild exultation thrilling me, then reached up my rifle and edged
forward again. I heard voices. Two of the Senussiyeh were speaking, and I could understand their Egyptian Arabic well enough.

"You will be relieved at dawn, brother," said one. "The *mokaddem* commands that we bear off certain of these jewels, together
with the Prophet, whom may Allah bless!"

"And the infidel who escaped?" asked a second and deeper
voice.

"May he rot in hell!" exclaimed a third savagely. "By those
two shots we heard, he is lost in darkness. Guard these well, Ali,
and if they slip over the edge before dawn, so much the better.
Come, Muhammad!"

I heard footsteps, and slunk back beyond the bend, with my
rifle ready. Should those who were leaving come past me, there
would be no mercy. I was past showing mercy to these rats of
hell.

But they went on the other way, and when I peered forth
again their light was dim, and then vanished. Reckoning up, I
figured that since I had shot two of his men, the renegade still

had six left. From the conversation, and sound of steps, two of the three speakers had left this chamber, and one remained on guard.

Stepping to the doorway, I saw a strange tableau within the great chamber. Not far from the door was a pedestal in the floor, with a basin in the top—almost exactly the shape of a drinking fountain. In the basin was some kind of oil, and in the oil floated a burning wick, which gave a faint light.

To one side of the pedestal, leaning on his rifle, stood a *khuan* of the Senussiyeh—tall, sombre, motionless, and sinister in the flickering light. Beyond him and ranged against the farther wall there stood out very dimly a number of things which I took then for coffins. But I was after blood now, for from the talk I guessed that Solomon and Molly were confined in this chamber, and this must be the place of torture Parrish had discovered.

Yes, and I confess it without compunction, I was after blood. I could have downed the man easily enough; to shoot him was impossible, for it would have raised an alarm above, since they had heard my two previous shots. So I simply stole up behind the man and brained him, reversing my rifle.

I rather believe, in cold blood, that the deed requires the half-apology I had given for it.

In any case, it was done, and done thoroughly. The man dropped without a sound to the stones. Leaning over him, I took away his rifle, caught a revolver from his belt, found more dried dates and a flask of water, and also a new electric flash-lamp. Then with a grunt of satisfaction, I settled down to make a meal.

God forgive me for the time I wasted there! When I had eaten and drunk, I rose and went to the farther wall, taking the flash lamp because of the dim light thrown by the pedestal lamp. And when I reached those coffin-like objects a great surprise came to me.

They were not coffins at all. They were stone boxes, and the one directly before me was half filled with dusky jewels!

What was in the other boxes I never knew or cared. Plunging

my hands into those jewels, I caught up some of them, mad with excitement, and filled the pocket inside my woollen burnoose. I was still staring and reaching for more like a child after jam, when a terrible whispered cry seemed to fill the chamber.

" 'Ang on, miss! Doctor Firth is some'heres about."

"Solomon!" I whirled with a mad cry. "John! Where are you?"

"Oh, God, 'e's come!" and I shall never forget the awful cry of heartfelt thankfulness in those words. "We're 'ere, sir! 'Urry!"

The voice came from my right, and I swept the light over that end of the big chamber. It was quite blank and bare, the abode of emptiness itself. There was nothing but bare walls and floor.

CHAPTER XII

THE PIT

LET ME place this much to my credit: From the moment I heard John Solomon's voice I forgot all about those jewels, and I never thought of them again until long afterward.

Sweeping the light about the place, I tried vainly to locate someone. The voice had come from somewhere in that very room, yet no person was in sight.

"Where are you?" I cried out, horrified by the silence and emptiness.

"Over this way, sir," came John's gasping cry. "Step this way, sir—'urry!"

There was urgency in that exhausted voice, and I advanced toward it. Then, as I swept the light across the floor, I saw that pit of hell.

It was a circular basin in the floor, twenty feet from edge to edge at the top. The sides sloped slightly, exactly like the sides of a funnel; that is precisely what it was—a huge funnel. Further, the sides were smooth, and were lined with glazed tiles, which made them like glass.

The bottom of the funnel was a black hole, to which I paid no attention then. Around the rim, a yard down from the floor of the chamber, were set a circular row of great stone hooks. Each of them curved up, like meat hooks, being some six inches or more long. Upon that, I perceived dimly what the thing was and meant.

With the cords of his bound wrists hung around one of those

stone hooks, John Solomon was suspended directly beneath me, his staring eyes looking up from a bloodstained and agonised face. From the second hook, six feet around the circle, hung Molly Quaintance in the same fashion; but she had fainted mercifully.

"Give me your 'and!" gasped John.

He tried to squirm upward against the slippery tiling, only to relax with a groan. I knelt hastily, but could not reach down to him, so pulled off my burnoose and lowered it. With an effort, he grasped the stout cloth, and a moment later I gripped his bound wrists and jerked him over up the edge, like a fish out of the water.

I paused for no explanations, but hurriedly ran around to where Molly was suspended. This time I took chances, for my heart was in my throat, and I leaned down till I could grip the poor girl's nerveless fingers. I had been forced to leave the light on the floor; by the reflection from the glazed tiles I could see the pitiful beauty of her dark face, and it struck to my heart.

Slowly I lifted her, and finally brought her up over the edge of the floor; Solomon was beside me.

"I 'ave me penknife in me pocket, Doctor Firth," he said calmly, though his face was streaked with bloody sweat. "If so be as you'll—"

Reaching into his pocket, I got the knife and freed him and Molly from their bonds. Then I went back to the pedestal, got what was left of the dead man's flask of water and dates, and brought them over. Solomon was sitting with Molly's head in his lap, and, after putting a little of the fluid between her teeth, we brought her around.

My desperate fear lest she had been injured lessened when she sat up and looked at me. There was a wild wonder in her face, and, without a word, I took her into my arms and held her so; I could feel the flutter of her heart against my breast, but my own heart was too full for speech.

"We knew you would come, Walter," she said at length, quite simply.

"That's more than I did," and I essayed a shaky laugh. "Heaven only knows how I ever got here—"

"That's right, Doctor Firth," broke in Solomon. "That's quite right! Yes, sir and miss, that's right. 'Eaven knows a mortal lot, I says, as no man ain't going to know till 'e gets there 'isself. Thank God, says I, for bringfn' of you 'ere in 'Is own way!"

"Amen to that," I said, ashamed, and caught at his hand. "John, I'd give a good deal if I had your quiet, undoubting faith!"

"Look after John, Walter," urged Molly before he could reply. "I'm afraid he's badly hurt, though he protested he was all right."

Solomon tried to protest the same thing now, but I would have none of it. While Molly held the flash lamp, I examined him, and found that aside from a bruised face and cut scalp he was sound enough. Parrish's kicks had only bruised him slightly.

"What time is it?" I asked suddenly.

"Close on midnight, sir," and John shivered as he looked at the pit. "Beggin' your pardon, Doctor Firth, but we'd best move away from that 'ere place. If fair gives me the creeps, as the 'ousemaid said when the old gentleman—"

What the old gentleman did I never knew, for I had remembered the dead man. Hastily rising, I strode over and dragged him into the darkness, spreading out his brown burnoose for all of us to sit upon.

"Now," I said, when we were settled, and John was whittling at his plug tobacco, "what's next? Where is Parrish, and what has happened? Did I hurt him much?"

"Smashed 'is jaw, sir," and John chuckled gravely. "Werry mad 'e is, Doctor Firth. There's no use a-doing anything till daybreak, sir."

"Why till daybreak? Won't that camel bring down your men to the rescue?"

"Werry simple, Sir. That 'ere blooming camel, 'e went off by another bridge, so we can't depend on 'im, sir. But I'd arranged with me men that if I needed 'em, why, I'd send up a bit o' smoke, just like that. So we'll 'ave to wait till daybreak, says I."

"So you'd arranged to summon your men by a smoke signal?" I repeated. "Why the devil didn't you tell me so before?"

"I didn't 'ave no chance, sir," he returned meekly.

I grunted. "Well, we're up against it, because we can't send any smoke from here. Parrish has the body of your precious Prophet—"

"No, sir," broke in John stolidly, and nodded at my stare. "No sir and miss, we ain't up against it, beggin' your pardon. If so be as I can get a bullet into that 'ere corpse, why, Parrish 'e's up against it."

Whereupon he condescended to explain at length why I found him stripped to his linen *kamis*. After I had made my break, Parrish, with a broken jaw, had done what he could for his own hurts, and had then proceeded to take vengeance. Before bringing Molly and Solomon down here, he had taken John's burnoose and wrapped up the body of Muhammad in it. The point to all this was that in John's burnoose there were two sticks of dynamite.

"By thunder!" I exclaimed, feeling weak suddenly. "Was that stuff on you when he was kicking you around?"

"It was that, sir," and John puffed away at his old clay, which had miraculously survived.

"All right, go ahead," and I waved my hand helplessly. "I guess the day of miracles isn't past yet, that's all!"

"No, sir, it's not," assented John solemnly.

Molly had suffered no insult, beyond being bound and left in that pit. This was explained by the severe monastic rules of the Senussiyeh, which, as I have before set forth, had lifted Parrish and his men into a machine-like disregard of all emotion or personality or pity.

Therefore, the situation at present was somewhat complicated. We were in the hole, and couldn't get out; Parrish was out, and couldn't get in—without our killing one or two of his five remaining men. We had two rifles and one revolver. He had the body of Muhammad, and knew nothing about the two sticks of dynamite.

"So he hung you up by the hands there, eh?" And I chafed the pretty wrists of Molly. She shivered a little.

"He—he told us about the place first," she faltered. "It was horrible!"

"You go an' take a look at that 'ere pit, Doctor Firth," said John. "Clear to the bottom, just like that. You don't know it all, an' a werry good job as you don't, as the old gentleman said when 'e married 'is third."

"Why, what's there?" I asked in surprise. Molly only turned and loosened my hands, so I took the flash-lamp and went.

Peering down the edge of that horrible chute, at first I could make out nothing except that it was some twenty feet to the hole beneath. The point of the torture was, it seemed, to hang the victims by the hooks until the agony grew so intense that of their own will they would loosen the clutch of the cords and go.

I looked at the pictured tiles which lined the hell-hole. Then, at thought of Molly, I grew rather sick, and made out what was below. The hole at the bottom was six feet across, and, perhaps, ten in depth. Once it had been far deeper than that. Sticking up to the top of it were long, slender spikes, some of them broken off. They may have been made of copper or bronze, for they had not rusted away, and piled up around them at the bottom were bones and skulls.

It was very simple and horrible. The victim, when at length he let go, slid down and was pierced by one or two of those thin spikes, sliding down of his own weight, and writhing there until he died. Getting out was impossible.

Feeling a bit faint at thought of how I had calmly been eating and drinking at the other end of that room, while Solomon and Molly hung there, I retreated and came back to them, wiping the cold sweat from my face. Molly did not look at me, but John did, and after one look he puffed at his pipe in silence. I did not care to speak myself for a bit, but filled my own pipe.

Molly must have been wearied to death. When I looked at her again, I found that she had curled up beside us on the wide burnoose, and was sound asleep. I glanced at John, and he beckoned me to one side with a jerk of his head. I followed him out of the door of the passage-way, where he drew a ring from his finger and gave it to me.

"Take this 'ere ring, sir. It may come in 'andy, so to speak."

"Eh?" I held it up, and found it to be a small ring of silver, engraved with some odd device. "What for?"

"Well, it may come in 'andy," he repeated. "Them 'ere men o' mine don't know you or Miss Quaintance, sir. If so be as you should meet up with 'em, this 'ere ring will make all right and tight. They knows it, sir."

I looked at him for a moment, but his eyes were wide and quite devoid of any expression.

"What do you mean, John? You're going to get off with us, of course?"

"That's me 'ope and intention, sir, as the 'ousemaid said when the old gentleman asked 'er to be marry in' of 'im." John hesitated, and I could see a little straggle in his face, then he turned to me and laid a hand on my arm: "I 'ave a feeling, Doctor Firth, as 'ow summat mortal bad's a-going to 'appen to me. It—"

"Nonsense, man!" I pulled myself into my best professional manner. "It's the effect of the strain you've been through, and this damned place. Go over there and lie down beside Molly, and get some sleep. I'll stand watch at the door here."

"Yes, sir," he said quietly. "But don't you forget about that 'ere ring."

"Wait a minute," I said, as he turned. "Where are we; do you know?"

"Not werry far inside the entrance under the big cross, sir. Five or six doors down the passage, mebbe."

"Whew!" I looked at him with a long whistle. "Well, get along with you."

"One word, sir. I'm 'ere to blow up that 'ere corpse. If I don't do it, I want your word of honour that you'll do it, sir."

"I'll blow up Muhammad and Parrish to boot, If I get the chance," I answered savagely.

"Werry good, sir," and he wagged his head as he looked at me. "Doctor Firth, if so be as anything 'appens to me, will you be so good as to lay me under that 'ere cross, where Muhammad was put? It'd be a mortal lot o' comfort, sir, to think as 'ow I'd be a-layin' there—"

"Confound it, man, you're bilious!" I shot out half-angrily. "I'll do anything you say, if you go over there and sleep."

"Thankee, sir." He bobbed his head, tiptoed over to the pedestal, and lay down beside Molly.

Smoking to keep myself awake, I leaned on my rifle and stood in the doorway. To tell the truth, weariness had all but conquered me; yet I was fully awake to the necessity of keeping guard. Those men had said something about Parrish getting the jewels, so he or his men might be down at any moment. If he came by himself, all would be simple; we could get hold as hostage, get through his men—and then shoot him.

However, that seemed like a slim hope. After a little I caught myself nodding, and in rank fear I got out my flash-lamp. John had said we were close to the entrance, therefore I could get some water, and a wash would keep me awake.

Flashing the light only to make sure that the way ahead was clear, I stepped out, and, after a dozen steps, found myself in a wide corridor. Then at last I knew where I was. After tumbling down those steps, I had taken the right hand of two passages; now I was in the opening of the left hand passage. Out ahead I could catch a dim star glow, and slowly walked across to the other passage, now sure of myself.

There was no mistake, for I found the water puddle and enjoyed a drink and a good wash, after filling the flask which I had fetched from the chamber. Then I sat down and pondered a terribly strong temptation.

I could do several things. By reaching the top of the stairway I could either plant a bullet in Muhammad and blow up the whole crowd—myself included—or I could open fire on Parrish and his five men, or I could steal off and bring the Nejd men to the rescue. After thinking it over, I stayed where I was—I had done enough running away for one time, I concluded.

Just as I rose to my feet, a thought struck me with stunning force. After an instant I turned and put for the torture chamber again, filled with excitement. John had had an hour's sleep, so without compunction I roused him without waking Molly. He came over to the doorway, and I told him about finding that room where they had made the tiles in centuries past.

"Now," I concluded, "if we stay here we're up against it hard, John. Parrish will come down, and either blockade us or shoot us up, and we've no food or water to speak of. On the other hand, if we dig out of here, we'll be out of reach.

"And something else, John. There's a furnace in that the place—get that? I didn't see anything to burn, but we can find bones almost anywhere, and bones will send out a pretty good smoke about daylight. How does it strike you?"

John's eyes lit up and he nodded.

"And just where might that 'ere place be, Doctor Firth?"

"Oh, we'll find it," I said excitedly. "I don't know exactly where it is, but there'll be no trouble in rummaging around—"

"No, thankee," he declared emphatically. "Gettin' lost is a werry good thing sometimes, sir, as you've been an' proved, but this 'ere ain't the time, says I. Beggin' your pardon, sir, but we'll stay right 'ere an' take what comes, just like that. Now you go get a bit o' sleep, sir. I've 'ad me bit, and you look mortal tired, for a fact."

I made no bones about admitting it. While somewhat disappointed that he had so quickly squelched my brilliant idea, I realized that at bottom he was correct. It was better to endure the ills we had than to go skirmishing for others that we knew not of. So I directed John to the water supply, gave him my flash lamp, and lay down beside Molly, who was still sound asleep.

Being dog tired, I was off almost instantly. As I discovered later, Solomon stood sentry for three hours: then I wakened to find his hand on my shoulder. He had so much trouble arousing me that Molly also came up, rubbing her eyes.

"Quiet, sir and miss!" whispered John quickly. "Better come to the door wi' me, sir. There's someone a-coming."

Springing up, I seized my rifle, patted Molly's cheek, and followed John to the entrance. There was a straight view to the main passage, and at the end I caught the flicker of a light and the sound of slow steps.

"One man," I commented quickly. "Wait a moment."

Returning to Molly, I motioned her back into the darkness out of sight, and picked up the burnoose of the dead man; I put it on and drew up the hood, then took my position, rifle in hand, by the pedestal. In that dim light Parrish would take me for the guard-and I was going to get him this time for keeps. That it was Parrish I had no doubt in the world, but in any case I would get the visitor. After seeing that pit, I wanted more blood.

"Get back," I whispered and Solomon obeyed as he caught my plan.

A moment later the steps had come to the door-way; I turned slightly, and caught sight of the bandaged visage of Parrish, saluted, and stood at attention. He seemed to feel something wrong, paused for a moment, then, without a word, walked in. We had trapped him!

CHAPTER XIII

FAIR WEATHER

THE RENEGADE could not talk, of course, having a broken jaw. His suffering must have been intense, and I was savagely glad of it.

After he had passed me I drew up my rifle and cocked it. The click caught his attention, and he turned, but I remained immobile, and, after a glance, he went on. His own flash-lamp swept out and rested on the coffin-like stone cases ranged along the wall. He had come for the jewels, after all!

None of us made a sound. Being quite sure of him, I was willing to play with him to the end; pity or mercy was as far out of my mind as it was out of his. So, in grim silence, I watched him while he stood before the cases and let the jewels stream between his fingers in a flaming cascade.

Swiftly he began to crowd them into his pockets and must have filled his burnoose. This done, he turned and sent the finger of light streaming across the pit as he advanced toward it. As the crucial moment was almost upon us, I turned to the blackness behind me and motioned as if pressing a flash-lamp. I caught a slight sound, and knew that John had understood the gesture. My rifle came up.

I had no intention of killing Parrish at the moment, but had to make sure of him. He slowly advanced to the edge of the pit, and his light quavered down into it as he leaned over, trying to make out the farther depths below. Then, with a swift motion, he whirled and flashed his light over in my direction-he had discovered the escape! At the same instant John's flashlight struck and held him.

"Better not," I said quietly, as he jerked at his revolver. "Hands up!"

Wisely enough, he reached for the ceiling. I had him covered, and he knew better than to tempt my bullet.

"Go, tie him up, John," I went on. "Mind you do the job thoroughly. Bring him over here, and we'll tie his feet, then rope him to the pedestal here."

I was curious to see how Parrish took his defeat, but by reason of the bandage enveloping his jaw and face I could make out nothing except his cold venomous eyes. John bound his wrists with some of the same cords I had cut from him and Molly, and pushed him toward us. Molly had come to my side.

"You're not going to—to shoot him, Walter?" she murmured.

"Not just yet," I whispered grimly. "He's got to serve as hostage, Molly. Never you mind what I say to him, though."

She drew back, and Parrish came into the circle of weird light cast by the pedestal lamp. He walked very firmly, carried himself erect and straight, and over the bandage his terrible eyes met mine with never a quiver.

The blow must have been a terrific one to him; for as I have said, the man was undoubtedly sincere in working for his devilish monastic order. His one thought was to serve Islam. We had turned the tables on him in the very moment of victory—in fact, had repeated his own coup of the morning before. He could have expected no mercy, and all his schemes had crashed down to failure, yet he bore himself more regally than ever, and could he have talked, I make no doubt that his words would have been edged with vitriol, as of old. Talk he could not, however.

When John had taken the revolver from his holster, Parrish stood and watched us, hands bound behind him. He was like a king at bay; helpless and broken as he was, I still feared him and he knew it. The consciousness that he knew it stung me.

"You had to come after the jewels, eh?" I sneered at him.

"Wanted loot, didn't you? Well, you've lost loot and all this time. Parrish."

My insinuation was unfair, but I wanted to reach under his hide, and I did it. He tried hard to speak, for I saw his knotted neck muscles straining in agony; but the bandage gagged him well enough, and the effort must have been painful in the extreme.

"Beggin' your pardon, Sir," broke in John, shuffling forward, "but it's gettin' on toward dawn, Doctor Firth. While you're 'olding of 'im, as a 'ostage, so to speak, I might be goin' up above and light a bit o' fire to call in me men."

This was the first intimation Parrish had that we were not alone. He started slightly, and his eyes went to Solomon.

"Where are your men, then?" I asked. "There are four causeways, it seems."

"Yes, sir. We come in from the northwest, but me men are waitin' over by the southwest corner, sir. Colonel Parrish, 'ere, must 'ave come in from the southeast bridge, 'cause why, we didn't see none o' them motor-buses on our side."

For the first time I caught a swift gleam of apprehension flit across the cold brown eyes of the renegade, and I knew that Solomon had figured aright. At this juncture Molly's hand fell on my arm, and I turned to her.

"Look after his face, Walter," she begged me, an intent seriousness in her own sweet features. "He was in terrible pain after you left, and—"

"So much the better," I said calmly. "The more he suffers, the better I'll be pleased, dear!"

"Don't say that!" she cried, sharply. "It's not like you, Walter! No matter what he has done, it's your duty to do what you can to relieve him."

I looked into her eyes for a moment, and the shamed the brute in me.

"I beg your pardon, dear," I said softly, and turned. "Solomon, you keep Parrish covered. I'm going to set his jaw for him, if it's not done already. That is, of course, if he's willing."

The renegade, who had heard Molly's words, nodded quietly. While John held a rifle at his back, I stepped forward and took off the bandage.

Never have I seen such iron fortitude as Lionel Parrish displayed during those terrible moments. Molly could not watch it, and even John looked rather sick. My jab with the tile had opened his cheek to the bone, and the broken jaw had been merely tied up in slovenly fashion.

Though feeling absolutely no pity for the man, I tried not to hurt him through sheer force of habit. While I set the broken bone, he stood like a rock and uttered not a whimper; awful though the agony must have been, he gave no sign except the livid pallor which crept through his bronze, and the cold sweat on his face. I had no instrument, and could not stitch up the wound, but I made shift to leave him in far better shape than he had been previously.

"There's not much use in all this," I stated, when I was through at last. "You won't live very long if I have any say, my friend. However, there you are."

Thinking he was about to faint, I watched him curiously, but he gathered himself up and held firm. Then another idea came to me, and it was an excellent one; to this day I am convinced that if it had been carried out, the whole affair would have ended otherwise. I turned to Solomon.

"John, we had better give this devil a taste of his own medicine, and put him where he'll be safe in storage, as it were. Make sure of those cords about his wrists, then we'll hang him on one of those meat hooks yonder, while you call in your Nejd men. He'll be—"

"No, sir," interrupted John, mopping at his face. "No, sir! Not that."

"Eh? Why not?" I demanded. Parrish had not changed a hair. "You know perfectly well that we can't trust him. We'd better

both of us go up and build that fire, to make sure his men don't
try any tricks—and we'll build it out of Muhammad's body, if
you say the word."

John grimaced, and those last words drew a horrified stare
from the renegade. None the less, my suggestion was not in the
least prompted by cruelly or revenge. I did not want to let John
go up to the great pavement by himself, lest Parrish's men kill
him out of hand, and try to rescue their leader by rushing me;
nor did I want Molly to take any chances by accompanying us
up.

Our only hope was to play safe. By putting Parrish in that pit,
we could leave Molly here without danger; then, summoning the
Nejd men by making a smoke, we could return and wait till they
arrived. I explained all this at length, while Molly stood aside,
pale-faced and silent, and Parrish watched and listened grimly.
John, however, set himself firmly against the plan.

"No, sir," he repeated stubbornly. "I'm a Christian man,
Doctor Firth, and I won't use no danged contrivance like that
'ere pit. It ain't necessary, I says, just like that. This 'ere Parrish can
werry well be bound up 'and and foot, and left. We don't need
to fear 'im, sir, not with 'is broken jaw. Cruelty is all werry well,
says I, but it's werry bad when it ain't needful. I says no, just like
that, Doctor Firth."

More than once since then have I wished that I had settled
the whole matter out of hand by shooting Parrish where he
stood. And I think John would have assented to it. It was just
a bit beyond me, however, in Molly's presence; and after I had
found that John was fixed in his decision beyond any moving,
I gave up in disgust. If I had only over-ruled him, and forced
Parrish myself into the pit, how differently all might have come
out! But I did not, unfortunately.

"All right, have it your own way, then," and I took the strap
from my rifle. "Strip up that burnoose, John, and at least we'll
tie him up beyond any question of his escape."

There was more than a hint of scorn in the dark eyes of

Parrish, and even in that moment I verily believe that he was anticipating his triumph. What a man he was! If there was ever a devil out of hell who walked this earth, it was Lionel Parrish, prefect of the Senussiyeh, renegade Christian, leader of the Islamic menace in the East, and once, save the mark, an American officer.

John had taken away his revolver, and I never thought to look for a second weapon, by some evil chance. When we had the burnoose of the man whom I had killed stripped up, we made Parrish stand against that pedestal lamp, his back to it. The top of the basin came at just the right height to bind his wrists, as he stood.

Parrish must have filled that basin with oil while he awaited our coming, though where he found the oil I have no idea. It was still burning, being only half-used up, and the cloth wick was floating about as it burned.

Watching John knot those cords, my fears of Parrish vanished slowly. His wrists were firmly bound to the rim of the basin, then his body; after which John fastened ankles and knees in like manner to the pedestal, and knotted the lines with all the skill of a seaman. Inspecting the job with the flashlight, I could have sworn that nothing short of a miracle would liberate the man; even his elbows were bound down to his sides, and drawn together behind. I forgot that John himself had said the days of miracles were not over.

"A werry good job, sir and miss," declared John, and calmly drew forth his plug and knife and old clay pipe.

I nodded, satisfied, and turned to Molly.

"You won't be afraid if we leave you, dear? We'll send up a smudge and be right down again."

She put up her face to mine for a moment, brave-eyed.

"No, Walter. I—I'll try not to be afraid. But hurry back, please!"

I assured her that we would do so, caught up my rifle, and accompanied John to the passage entrance. I looked back once to see Parrish standing grim and straight in his bonds, and Molly gave me a wan smile of farewell; then we left the dread chamber and were in the passage.

John requested me to leave the talking to him, and we made no effort to conceal our steps as we came to the stairway. With a surge of emotion I saw the blessed daylight once again, and drew in a deep breath of the fresh morning air.

The renegade's men were on the alert. As we reached the stairway at the end of the passage, a brown-clad figure at the top whirled upon us with uplifted rifle. John threw up his hand and spoke quickly in Arabic:

"Do not fire! We come in peace."

With a wondering scowl the man inspected us while we ascended, then turned and called his four companions. They crowded forward with rifles ready, and broke into guttural exclamations of amazement at sight of us. John, puffing at his pipe, addressed them without fear:

"Stay where you are. Your *mokaddem* is a prisoner in our hands. At the first shot, or if one of you try to descend those stairs, he dies. Remember that, brethren of dogs."

The information staggered them. They could not doubt its truth, else we had never walked so openly into their hands, and we had them neatly. They dared not shoot us lest Parrish be slain, so they gathered off to one side in a sullen group.

John turned to me calmly, and pointed out the position of the Neid men. Standing with the great cross and stairway behind us, we faced due south. We had come from the northwest causeway, behind us and to our right. At the diametrically opposite corner of the great quadrangle, facing us and to our left, was the southeast causeway down which our camel had gone, and by which Parrish and his men had come. To our right was the south-western bridge, at the far end of which the Nejd men were encamped. The cross, of course, stood in the centre of the whole pavement.

A strong wind was coming down from the western desert—

hot and dry, waving the brown canes and strewing part of the huge rock with red flowers. Those flowers must have been parasitic, for the canes were quite dry, many of them broken by the stiff desert wind. The sun had been up about an hour, I calculated.

"Gettin' ready to carry Muhammad off, they were," observed John, pointing.

They must have worked hard at the job, too. A quantity of the canes had been cut and lashed together very strongly and neatly into a sort of litter. For the little band to carry off the stone sarcophagus was, of course, out of the question, and the litter lay in front of the opening, with the body of Muhammad upon it, still covered by the burnoose taken from Solomon.

It struck me that John made an odd figure, in his torn, dirtied, bloodied *kamis* and his sandalled feet, his pudgy little figure looking more like a caricature than anything else. He squinted up at the sky, then glanced around.

"Doctor Firth, that 'ere wind is out o' the northwest, ain't it?"

"It is," I assented. "Why?"

"Nothing at all, sir," and he knocked out his pipe with a sigh. "Well, sir, if you'll get some o' them odds and ends o' cane together, we'll send up a smoke as'll call in me men."

Going over to the litter, I gathered up some scraps of cane which had been cut by the men, and brought them to the stairway. They were very brown and dry, and John examined a strip of cane carefully, piercing midway between the joints with his knife. A few drops of water ran from each.

"Do that wi' them all, sir," he ordered. "You see, I told them 'ere Arabs as 'ow Parrish'd be shot if there was any shootin' up 'ere. Well, them canes will explode like pistols, sir, 'aving water in 'em. We 'ave to mind them 'ere Arabs, sir."

I nodded and pierced the joints one by one, then made a little pile of the canes, stripping one into shreds first. To this I touched one of my few remaining matches, and the stuff blazed up instantly with a thick smoke. The five Arabs watched us in black suspicion, but they dared make no offensive move.

"That's enough, sir," said John, as the smoke rose high. "Let 'er bum out, and we'll be gettin' back. I 'ave me doubts—"

"Why not put a bullet into Muhammad now?" I suggested. He shook his head in negation, looking over at the litter and body.

"No. It'd only set a flame to these 'ere Arabs, sir. 'Urry's a werry good thing in its place, says I, but this ain't its place. Let's get back, sir."

He seemed uneasy and nervous, so with a final glance around, I joined him, and we started down the stairs. John chuckled suddenly.

"If so be as they make a bolt for it, sir, there's one werry good way o' stopping them."

"What is it?" I inquired, wondering at his manner.

"Why, sir, they'd go right off down that 'ere south-east cause-way toward the machines as fetched 'em 'ere. We go off by that 'ere sou'west causeway to me own men. Wi' the wind out o' the north-west, sir, a bit o' fire in them canes—" He paused suddenly and gripped my arm. We were in the passage, and a faint cry came to us from beyond, a wail in Molly's voice:

"Walter! Help—help—"

Solomon darted ahead of me like a rabbit, his rifle flung up.

CHAPTER XIV

THE LAST MATCH

NEVER SHALL I forget the scene that met my eyes as I came to the doorway of the torture chamber.

A pungent, horrible odour of burning flesh swirled out, and almost sickened me, even while I flashed forth the light in my left hand, my drawn revolver in my right. Parrish was still standing against the pedestal, but Molly was clinging frantically to him, and shaking him unavailingly, for he stood like a rock.

In some inexplicable fashion, although unable to free his hands, he had slipped up the cords over the edge of the oil basin. Then coldly deliberate as ever, he had held his wrists down to the flame until his cords had been burned away. The first Molly had known of it was when she smelled the burning flesh, and then, instead of striking out the flame in the basin, she had flung herself on Parrish in wild panic and shrieked for us.

Just as I came into the doorway, the renegade's hands came free, and he flashed out a knife. Solomon had beaten me to the room, but dared not fire for fear of hitting Molly. Now, as the poor girl went staggering back, John closed with Parrish in desperation, and yelled at me to shoot.

It was useless, for Solomon was of absolutely no use in a physical encounter, and Parrish paid no heed whatever to his blows, but stooped swiftly and freed his legs with a slash of the knife. Molly had fallen to the floor, and as the renegade came up I tried a snapshot with my revolver; but I had been running, and so missed him clean. He gave a leap, dragging John with him, then jerked out a revolver and brought it down with a thud on John's skull.

Meantime, I had been running in upon him, wild fury in my heart—for the entire affair passed in a flash, though now it takes long to tell of it in proper sequence. As his pistol fell on John, I shot again at two yard's distance and hit, for I saw him stagger; then he fired point-blank at me and caught up the body of John as a shield.

Now, account it superstition or Providence or the hand of God, as you will, the only thing which saved my life in that moment was the tile I had kept in my burnoose pocket—the crimson tile marked with the word "Theos," the Greek for God. The bullet struck it and glanced away, but the shock drove the tile into my stomach and doubled me up for one agonized instant.

I think Parrish believed me dead, and Molly also, for he did not shoot again. Still holding the body of John like a shield, he darted to the door; my light had fallen from my hand, and in my case I dared not fire again. Follow I could, however, and I tried desperately to catch him in the corridor outside.

But, wounded and broken as the renegade was, his tremendous strength showed itself. Carrying John Solomon like a child, he drew ahead of me down the passage, and desperately I fired after him, trying to hit his legs and cripple him. But a flashing report echoed back from the main passage leading to the stairway, and, with a sobbing curse, I stumbled back again. Parrish's men had come down, and the renegade had escaped with John dead or wounded, and captive.

Coming so hard upon our exultation, the thing numbed me, paralysed me. It seemed incredible. If we had only hung Parrish by one of those bronze hooks in that hell pit! Yet I remember quite clearly that my great regret was for John himself; we in the chamber were safe enough, but his fate seemed certain.

I staggered into the chamber and leaned on the pedestal, unnerved and sobbing, utterly heedless of Molly. Oh, if I had but shot Parrish like the dog he was, instead of trying to make use of him! Never until then did I fully realize how I loved John Solomon—loved him for his absurdities, loved him for his stout heart and wise soul and simple, sturdy uprightness. And now he was as good as dead.

"Curse you, Parrish—curse you!" I screamed out hoarsely, and, wiping the tears of rage and grief from my eyes, I caught up the rifle at my feet where John had dropped it. My wild paroxysm of blind rage carried me to the door with no better intent than to rush after the renegade and shoot him down ere his men killed me.

"Walter—Walter, are you mad?"

I was halted by Molly's voice, and her arms clung frantically around my neck, for she must have realized my mad purpose. And for the moment I was crazed, because I struggled against her, cursing frenziedly and striving to tear loose her arms. But I could not, and at length shame of my own brutality came over me, and with a groan I relaxed.

"Be quiet, dear," she pleaded shakily, terrified and almost beside herself, yet keeping a far clearer head than I. "Remember, I've got only you, dear! Be careful, dear Walter, for my sake!"

She could have used no firmer argument. Trembling still, I took her silently into my arms; I realized the madness she had saved me from, and the love which had prompted her, and I pressed my lips to her hair in gratitude that I had not myself harmed her.

"It's all right, dearest," I said brokenly. "Let me go, now."

I picked up the electric torch, gave it to her, and went to the doorway. A buzz of voices came from far down the passage, and I waited and listened, while calmness came back to me, and new poise. Presently I heard John's voice, in Arabic:

"It will do no good, but I will speak with him.—Give me the message."

I knew that they were sending him back, and took new hope. More inarticulate voices, then one of the Arabs spoke out:

"Swear by the cross of your faith that you will return."

"I swear," said John, and then footsteps came toward me. A moment later he lifted his voice:

"Doctor Firth! Doctor Firth!"

"Here I am, John," I made answer.

He came up to me in the darkness, and I gripped his hand in heartfelt anxiety. But he would make no reply to my questions concerning his well-being.

"Listen 'ere, sir," he said hoarsely. "Parrish, 'e means to get me out o' this and kill me slow, so to speak—'E says to you, sir, as 'ow 'e is willing to spare me if so be as you'll keep them Nejd men off 'is track."

"You mean," I asked, "that he'll keep you as hostage, that he'll spare you if the Nejd men let him safely away?"

"So 'e says, sir, but 'e lies," whispered John. "Don't bother wi' that 'ere offer, sir, 'cause why, 'e ain't to be trusted, as the 'ousemaid said about the old gentleman. I'm a-going back to 'im, Doctor Firth, and—"

"For God's sake, don't!" I groaned. "Break your promise and stay here, John—"

"Doctor Firth, don't talk like that!"

He cried out the words sharply, so that I glimpsed the struggle within him, and was rebuked. He was no breaker of faith, was John Solomon, even though he knew that Parrish's men were trying to give him false promises and hopes of safety.

"Now listen 'ere, sir," he whispered rapidly, "It don't matter about me, but it do matter about that 'ere body of Muhammad, sir. Them Nejd men are coming, and Parrish 'e knows it, so 'e's a-going to slip 'is cable in a mortal 'urry, sir. But you take your time, just like that."

"I understand," I said, as he paused, but in fact I did not understand. What he was aiming at I could not guess at all, and so waited for him to continue.

"Take your time, sir. We'll be gone in five minutes, then you and 'er go up above. Wait there for 'alf an 'our, close up that tomb if so be as you can do it, then—*fire them canes!*"

When at last I grasped his purpose, all my pleading was in vain. He cared absolutely nothing about his own fate, for he was centred wholly on the great cause to which he had given himself. Voices came calling to him from the Arabs, and he gripped my hands hard.

"Promise, Doctor Firth! You'll fire 'em?"

"Yes," I whispered. "I'll fire them. But John—John—is there no hope?"

He stood for a moment, silent.

"Yes," he answered, very hoarsely. "Yes, there's hope, Doctor Firth. Our Father, which art in 'Eaven—"

And with that he went stumbling away, back to those devils who awaited.

I do not know how they received him, for I returned to Molly, and a little later realized that I was holding her in my arms. She was asking me what we were to do, and her voice wakened me to myself. I told her John Solomon's last words.

"Now we're going to act, dear," I finished and kissed her solemnly.

John Solomon had left in my hands a legacy, and not alone a legacy of vengeance. Were Parrish to reach the mainland and his motor-sledges, the Nejd men would never catch him; the best racing camels in Arabia could not overtake those machines. He and his men were doubtless on their way by this time, for he would know the need of haste, and I trusted that he would hold Solomon as a hostage despite my refusal to accept his offer.

As John had said, there was no hurry. The south-eastern causeway, by which Parrish had come, was between ten and fifteen miles in length, as Solomon had explained to me while building the signal fire that morning. Also for nearly that whole distance it extended over the marsh, as the quicksand formed only a narrow strip in that quarter. What with wounds and the litter, the renegade and his men could not possibly proceed faster than a brisk walk, and I was safe in allowing them a good three hours and more before they could reach the mainland.

The Nejd men would be about the same length of time in reaching the square pavement, because it would be hard to get their camels over the stone causeway. I had ceased to think of them, however, save as a final means of escape. With each passing moment the scheme grew clearer to me exactly as Solomon must have mapped it out in his head at the last instant. Or had he planned it so from the very first, deliberately arranging that the dynamite should remain with Muhammad's body? That is something he never told me, but I would not deem it at all improbable.

"Wait here, dear, until I make certain they have gone," I said grimly enough, and quieted Molly's protest. "We're going to win John's greatest battle for him."

From that moment she put away all her distress and grief, and her fine character and self-reliance stood out in every word and deed. Until then she had, perhaps, unconsciously been dependent upon me and upon John, but more upon him, as was myself. Now, however, we must not shirk our work unless we were to let him die in vain, and the knowledge made us both move surely and capably.

Going to the main passage below the stairway, I paused and listened, but could hear nothing. It was not unlikely that Parrish was laying a trap for me, so I advanced up the stairway with my rifle ready.

Upon reaching the great pavement, I found it deserted, our little fire of canes fallen to ashes. From the hollow chamber in the cross pediment the empty sarcophagus grinned out at me in the silence; the litter had vanished, and Parrish had gone.

To another eye the place might have seemed very beautiful—the huge rock pavement white in the sunlight, enclosed by the gay walls and high waving reeds, with the great white cross towering up above. But to me it was hideously repellant. As I gazed out at that red sea of flowers topping the canes, waving wildly in the hot desert wind, it seemed to me that their ominous colouring had been a warning of the blood to be spilled in this place of horror.

And, too, the thought came to me of other things. By exploring this accursed Theopolis I might well find things undreamed of, for I had seen but a tiny part of all its rock-hewn mystery. Where there were caskets of jewels, there would be things far greater than jewels—

"Damn the place!" I cried aloud bitterly, and the hot desert wind swept the words off over the immense canebrake.

I could give Parrish half an hour—nay, wanted to give that much or more, that my vengeance might be the surer—on his way across the causeway. The scheme was diabolically certain, even without the dynamite wrapped up with the prophet of Islam. There was a gruesome diablerie in the thought of Muhammad's body destroying the men who had become devils in their service of him; perhaps it had appealed to John for that very cause, since he was a man who loved above all else to fit the punishment to the crime. Yet I do not know that the plan was intentional, after all.

Now, I calculated, there was no time to lose, for we were in the centre of that mile-square stone paving, and would have to reach our own causeway before starting our vengeance on the wings of the wind—vengeance, and death to John Solomon.

So leaving my rifle up above, I turned and retraced my steps to the chamber of horror. So many things had followed each other heel to toe that I was almost surprised to find that nothing had occurred during my absence. Molly was waiting for me, and I was glad to see that she was quite herself again.

"Come, dear—up into the daylight with you, and thank God that you'll never see this place again."

She looked into my eyes for a moment.

"Have *you* thanked Him, Walter?"

I had not, and in some shame I knelt and did so then and there, while Molly held my hand. Also, I prayed that John might yet come out alive, that his faith in God might be still further justified. Then we rose and sought the blessed daylight.

Remembering John's words, I set about closing the orifice in the cross pediment, sending Molly on ahead of me toward the southwest causeway. Picking up one of the tiles, I smashed it on the third copper boss as before. The mechanism worked, and I leaped back barely in time to escape the upward swing of the huge slab, as it swept into place with a smashing crash, and I saw the whole structure of the cross above shake with the terrific impact.

Feeling through my pockets as I ran, I set off hastily after Molly, not even pausing for my rifle. There was no time to waste, and I had just two matches, which John had given me for the signal fire that morning. I caught up with Molly a hundred feet from the causeway.

With that northwest wind coming down out of hell, I had only to light the canes on the leeward side of our causeway, and we would be in little danger. For a moment we paused and glanced back up against the blue sky, towered that gigantic, shattered cross, white and beautiful still, with the great pavement stretching around, and the high canes bordering all my dreams.

Reaching over the low stone wall along the edge of the causeway, I plucked a dry cane. Then in shelter of my body, I carefully struck one of my two matches; it went out. In desperate fear, I shredded out some of the cane, held it under my coat, and struck the other match. There was something terrible in the bare thought of what that match would do, and as the cane crackled up, I thrust the blackened stub in my pocket.

The cane burst out like a torch. As I thrust it into the tall mass to leeward, a joint exploded and I still see that plane in scattered sparks into all directions. In a flash a mass of flame had leaped up like a wall; I caught Molly's hand, and in swift panic over what I had done, broke into a run.

CHAPTER XV

THE JEWEL OF SENUSSI

A S MOLLY and I slowed down perforce into a walk, the triangle of cane to our left was being swept into a wild swirl of flame by the stiff wind. Between our causeway and that by which Parrish had gone was a solid cane-brake, stretching out for miles, and over all this the fire was spreading with the speed of lightning, it seemed.

The spectacle was appalling, as the mass of flame and smoke leaped high into the air, while a continuous fusillade took place as the water in the joints exploded under the heat; it was like a sham battle at Fort Myer; and what with the explosions and the increasing fury roar of the flames themselves, the quiet morning was transformed into a very inferno of sight and sound.

Now, the causeway was by no means straight, for at every half mile or so it twisted so that we could not see a great distance ahead. We must have come a mile when I began to appreciate that we ourselves were in danger.

"Speed up a bit, Molly," I exclaimed sharply. "That fire is eating down toward us, and it's pretty hot."

She stole an alarmed glance around, and we broke into a dogtrot. The flames, while driven away from us by the wind, were, nevertheless, travelling slowly down along the edge of the causeway as if in pursuit of us. They could do us no great harm save to give us a bit of scorching, but I was taking no chances.

And all the while I was listening—listening, every nerve taut and strained, every sense on the alert to catch some sound from the south-west. The leaping, roaring mass of flame must have travelled miles already, and from it there could be no escape, for it would overleap the causeway, and instantly incinerate any living thing upon it. Besides, there was the dynamite to consider.

Taken all in all, Parrish was doomed, and the body of Muhammad would perish from among mankind for ever. I wondered if John Solomon would ever know how that match had gone from his hand to accomplish his work—

"Look out, Walter!" cried Molly, and caught at my arm.

Hastily enough I followed her startled gaze, and some three hundred yards ahead, where the causeway shot off at an angle, I made out a large group of men on camels. In spite of the fact that the brutes hate stones above all things, the men rode at top speed, towering far above the causeway, and one of them bore a purple-and-orange flag. They were the Nejd colours, and these were the Nejd men; they had seen the fire, and were taking tall risks of their beasts falling, for they had seen the danger.

"Pull up, Molly," I said quietly.

As I spoke, a spat of fire darted from the foremost rider, and the bullet whistled above us. Recalling John's warnings and the ring he had given me, I stepped out and held up both my empty hands. There were fifteen of the camel men, and they tore at us like a whirlwind, but no more shots came at us.

As the riders approached, I plucked John's ring from my hand and held it up in the sunlight. They slowed down, and their leader, never waiting for his brute to kneel, slipped to the stones and ran to me. He was a fine-looking Arab, and after a moment I recognized him as the same whom I had seen in the room at Port Said with Solomon though all that seemed like uncounted ages ago.

"The ring of Suleiman!" I cried sharply, for he had half-raised his rifle. His men were already crowding in. The Arab gave me a sharp look, examined the ring, and slipped it on his own finger with a curt nod.

"Where is Suleiman?" he demanded. "Speak quickly, Nazarene!"

I did so, while Molly clung to my arm in no small fright at the circle of dark faces. I told them all that had happened, that John himself had commanded the reeds fired, and that he was with Parrish as a prisoner. Of Muhammad's body I said nothing, for the Arabs were ignorant of it; they thought that John was after some great buried treasure, because they were Moslems, and he had not dared tell them the truth.

"Good!" returned my acquaintance. "Let us return and see if any escape; you have but to command in the name of Suleiman, and it will be done. I remember having seen you at Port Said. By Allah, Suleiman cannot die this day!"

They all seemed stunned by my news, but turned about swiftly, for the beasts could no longer face the advancing flames and heat. Molly was ordered to one camel, and I was assigned to another, their owners being dismounted.

This was beyond us, however. Neither of us could ride the pitching brutes, and in the end we climbed up, each behind an Arab, and clung on as best we could to the rider. I chose the leader for my assistant, and we started toward the mainland.

"And these Senussiyeh dogs—they are on the south-east causeway?"

I assented, and he looked over the huge mass of flame and smoke to our left.

"There you speak truth, Nazarene. The camel of Suleiman was found last night, and we traced her track back to that causeway. Near it we found certain machines of Sheitan, where we left five men on guard. We saw the smoke this morning, and started to reach you—Allah curse our slowness!"

"It would not have mattered," I returned dully. "The thing was fated."

"Yes," he muttered into his beard. "It was fated. By the Prophet, Nazarene, if any of those Senussiyeh dogs escape the fire you have set after them, I swear that they shall meet a worse fate from my—"

He broke off sharply. Above the roar of the flames and the mad bursting explosions there had lifted a dull roar—a vibrating shock which needed no explaining. The dynamite had been reached!

"I fancy they won't escape," I returned dryly. "By the way, I'd like that ring back."

He grunted. "It is the ring of my master the emir."

That was answer enough for me, and I made no more demands. Our progress was by no means swift, for now that the need of haste was gone the Arabs would not hurry their choice beasts over the stones. From time to time I caught glimpses of Molly, clinging to her stately Arab, and she seemed to be getting on well enough.

So it was a good three hours before our slowly moving caravan debouched from the causeway to the mainland, and half a mile distant I sighted a cluster of low tents set up on a hillside near some palms. With great relief I realised that the ride was over; the racking pitch of the camel subsided, and as the brute knelt I leaped down and went to help Molly.

The whole group turned with us to watch that seething mass of flame rising above the great marsh. It was a tremendously impressive spectacle, for the fire had spread for miles above the canebrake, and the explosions had merged into a continuous roar that never died for an instant.

Suddenly the Arab leader caught my arm and pointed off to one side. I made out a tiny thread of smoke ascending against the blue sky, away from the fire.

"A signal from my five men at the end of the other causeway," he said. "Will you ride with us?"

I nodded, threw a reassuring word to Molly, climbed up behind him once more, and we were off. But I was far from feeling any exultation over the thing I had done, and now a swift alarm had wakened within me. Those five Nejd men on guard had not signalled for nothing. Was it possible that, despite fire and dynamite, the devil Parrish had won through, after all? Oddly, it never occurred to me that Solomon might be safe.

The very thought sent me into a sweat, for I still feared the renegade horribly, though I hated him far more. Ten of the Arabs were riding with us, and we were going at full speed; since five had been left on guard over Parrish's machines, I took hope. Even had he won through with all his men, five of those Nejd warriors, hatred in their hearts, would speedily have driven him off.

There had been no fight, however, as I discovered ten minutes later. We had covered some four miles of ground when a patch of riders was sighted ahead, coming toward us. There were five of them, and two camels bore double loads. With growing excitement I watched their approach—and knew the truth.

Parrish had won through! And so had John Solomon.

When our two parties met and exchanged reports, we learned that the renegade had come stumbling along the causeway; burned and wounded though he was, his iron fortitude and terrible spirit had carried him safe, though his men had perished. And after him had staggered poor Solomon, in desperate plight.

I knelt over him, for he was quite unconscious. The man was a mass of wounds; a broken rib from the renegade's kicks, a cut scalp, and one terrible knife slash across the calf of his right leg, which fortunately the Arabs had tied up. He had nearly bled to death as it was. I attended to this worst wound, then remembered Parrish and leaped up. And now, from across the circle of men, the renegade faced me coldly.

During a moment I could not speak for the surge of passions which had seized upon me. He was bound, fast, yet stood in all his arrogant pride; despite bandages, blood, and wounds, he looked more kingly than any man I have ever seen before or since.

"You know him?" said the Arab leader to me.

"Yes," and I think my voice shook. "He is djinn out of hell—he is Parrish Pasha, the man who would have slain Suleiman—who may yet die of his wounds. He is a prefect of the Senussiyeh."

One terrible growl went up from all those men—a growl with a horrible note of unleashed savagery ringing through it. No earthly power could save Parrish, and he knew it well. He glanced around the circle of savage faces and drew himself up as though in contempt; once more his piercing eyes settled on me, and then the Arab leader spoke:

"Shoot him!"

As I knelt over Solomon, I heard the rifles ring out over the roar of the flaming canes.

The Arab leader went to the renegade's body and stooped. Then he returned to me and gave me something heavy; it was a necklace of bronze, with a square pendant. In the centre of this was set a blazing ruby, and around the ruby was graven a device in Arabic. Somewhere I had seen that device ere this, and my mind went leaping back and back, until it settled on the wounded man whom I had first attended aboard ship.

I recalled the scene there in the cabin with the second officer and the dying stoker. I remembered the cicatrice upon the man's dark skin, and what Solomon had said about the later—the device of the Senussiyeh. I looked up at the tall Arab.

"What is this thing?" I asked slowly.

"It is the Jewel of Senussi, the grand master of this dog brotherhood," he snarled. "Ask me not how I know. Keep it or fling it away—" He turned on his heel.

I thrust the thing into my burnoose, along with the half-burned match and the loose gems, and so forgot if for that time.

The remainder of this record I will sketch briefly, for many things took place of which I have no room to write. My orders were obeyed implicitly, and after consulting with the Arab leader, I found that the quickest route to the outside world lay to the northeast. There we would find the French in Oman, and the Nejd men were on good terms with the tribes in that direction.

Inspecting the motor-carriages which Parrish had left, I

found that by combining what was left of petrol and supplies, we would have sufficient. So we visited the car Molly and I had left, picked it as the best of the three, and with the Arab leader and two men to guide and protect us, we started from Theopolis with no regret.

The trip to the coast took us a week, and it was the most terrible journey I have ever conceived. Solomon's wounded leg mortified despite all my care; at the first French station I was forced to amputate the leg at the knee. John refused anaesthetics, and gripped Molly's hand while I worked.

The French sent us on to Aden, where Molly and I were married, and with John we picked up a steamer. The loose gems I had carried from that hell-hole proved to be of no fabulous value, but they gave us a comfortable sum with which to start life together, and John, who was sadly broken, came home to America with us.

We came direct to Buffalo, where I found that one of my friends at Johns Hopkins was comfortably established in a good practice. Young Seaforth and I had always liked each other, so I bought into his practice and settled down, Solomon making his home with us. I have fixed him up with an artificial leg so that he gets around almost as well as ever. I have never dared even to show him the jewel of Senussi.

Yet the spell of the mysterious East is very strong upon me still. Two days ago, John received a letter and came into my study, pulling at his clay pipe. He was tremendously disturbed over something.

"Doctor Firth," he began cautiously, "I'm werry worry, sir, but I 'as to make a little trip."

"Yes!" I said. "Not far, John?"

"To New York, sir. I'd like werry well to 'ave you along, if so be as the missus don't object. I don't mind saying, sir, as 'ow there's prospects in view, as the old gentleman said when 'e saw the new 'ousemaid."

"I'll go to New York with you," I returned, searching

his inscrutable face. "But mind, no tricks! I'll not stir a step farther—"

"Yes, sir, werry good, sir," and he grinned a little as he went out.

I do not know what it means, but I go with him in three days.

To-day, as I close this record, I feel the "pull" of the East for some indefinite reason. Perhaps because of the three objects lying before me on my desk. One is the tile which saved my life—the crimson tile with the gold word "Theos" on its face. Beside it lies the bronze jewel of Senussi, the ruby glowing up at me dull red like the blood of murdered men. I must destroy the thing, for it has an uncanny influence, and I fear even to show it to John.

The third object is very small, and, like many small things, is very terrible. It is the blackened stub of a burned match, and when I think—

> Postscriptium Written by Cliff Seaforth, M.D.:
>
> It must have happened while Doctor Firth was closing up this record of his strange adventures. We found him stabbed in the left side, and the jewel he mentions as lying before him was gone. He is now in hospital and in no danger, but will not explain what happened. Nor will Mrs Firth.
>
> I do not like his silence, his long conferences with that ugly little Cockney named Solomon. Some emissary of that strange brotherhood, the Senussiyeh, must have tracked him unless indeed his whole record is a traveller's tale. Yet I think it is true. And I agree with my friend Firth that the burned match, with all it implies, is a terrible and significant thing.
>
> Query: Why does God always work through little, insignificant things such as burned matches and fat Cockneys?

ABOUT THE AUTHOR

H. BEDFORD-JONES is a Canadian by birth, but not by profession, having removed to the United States at the age of one year. For over twenty years he has been more or less profitably engaged in writing and traveling. As he has seldom resided in one place longer than a year or so and is a person of retiring habits, he is somewhat a man of mystery; more than once he has suffered from unscrupulous gentlemen who impersonated him—one of whom murdered a wife and was subsequently shot by the police, luckily after losing his alias.

The real Bedford-Jones is an elderly man, whose gray hair and precise attire give him rather the appearance of a retired foreign diplomat. His hobby is stamp collecting, and his collection of Japan is said to be one of the finest in existence. At present writing he is en route to Morocco, and when this appears in print he will probably be somewhere on the Mojave Desert in company with Erle Stanley Gardner.

Questioned as to the main facts in his life, he declared there was only one main fact, but it was not for publication; that his life had been uneventful except for numerous financial losses, and that his only adventures lay in evading adventurers. In his younger years he was something of an athlete, but the encroachments of age preclude any active pursuits except that of motoring. He is usually to be found poring over his stamps, working at his typewriter, or laboring in his California rose garden, which is one of the sights of Cathedral Cañon, near Palm Springs.

Printed in Great Britain
by Amazon

27057690R00088